'Are you flirting with me?'

'Was I not meant to?'

Ever since he'd appeared her emotions had been see-sawing dramatically as she struggled against a determination to keep him at arm's length—physically and emotionally—and an equally strong inclination to pull him close in every way.

'I don't want you!'

Before she knew it he was beside her. Without saying a word he planted one hand in the small of her back, the other on the curve of her hip, and with negligent ease dragged her to him.

She was too startled by his actions to resist. *That was her story and she was sticking to it!*

He arched an expressive brow and lowered his mouth to hers. His dark eyes glittered with insolent challenge. 'No…?'

Kim Lawrence lives on a farm in rural Anglesey. She runs two miles daily, and finds this an excellent opportunity to unwind and seek inspiration for her writing! It also helps her keep up with her husband, two active sons, and the various stray animals which have adopted them. Always a fanatical consumer of fiction, she is now equally enthusiastic about writing. She loves a happy ending!

Recent titles by the same author:

THE THORN IN HIS SIDE
A SPANISH AWAKENING

Did you know these are also available as eBooks?
Visit www.millsandboon.co.uk

IN A STORM
OF SCANDAL

BY
KIM LAWRENCE

First published in Great Britain 2011
by Mills & Boon, an imprint of Harlequin (UK) Limited.
Harlequin (UK) Limited, Eton House, 18-24 Paradise Road,
Richmond, Surrey TW9 1SR

© Kim Lawrence 2011

ISBN: 978 0 263 22132 9

Harlequin (UK) policy is to use papers that are natural, renewable and recyclable products and made from wood grown in sustainable forests. The logging and manufacturing process conform to the legal environmental regulations of the country of origin.

Printed and bound in Great Britain
by CPI Antony Rowe, Chippenham, Wiltshire

IN A STORM
OF SCANDAL

PROLOGUE

June 2004 Rome, Villa Palladio.

'You're a lucky man.'

'Yes I am, Uncle Dino.'

He *was* a lucky man.

Tell yourself that often enough, Luca, and it just might start to sound true.

Arranged marriages worked. The Ranieris had been making arranged marriages work for generations.

His own grandparents' marriage cementing two powerful Italian families had been arranged, maybe not such a good example…but his own parents had continued the custom and with some success.

But he had always considered himself the moderniser destined to drag his family into the twenty-first century.

However, a lot could change in six weeks.

It had been six weeks to the day when he had accepted his father's seemingly innocent suggestion to join him for a brandy in his study.

After first pouring them both a generous measure of brandy Damiano Ranieri had extracted a box from the safe concealed behind a painting before ceremoniously presenting it to his son.

'It was your great-grandmother's, Luca.'

It seemed supremely ironic now to recall that when he had stared at the heirloom sitting in its bed of velvet his first thought had been: *he knows…somehow he knows about us. He knows about Poppy!*

He knows and he isn't screaming or even threatening to disown me!

Touched by what he had seen—for about thirty seconds—as an unexpected parental display of approval, he had opened his mouth to tell his father how much he appreciated the gesture, but that would have been slightly premature.

He and Poppy had discussed the future and envisaged spending it together but they had both agreed that they were too young to make that sort of commitment yet.

'See how you feel after we've spent the next year together, Luca?' Poppy had teased as they sat beside the loch, and planned the route of their gap-year expedition. 'By then you might have gone off me totally.'

After he had demonstrated that he was never going to go off her—a task that took some time as her mouth was an invitation to sin—Luca had tugged the sides of his shirt together across his chest and growled. 'And you'll have moved on, basking in the attention of all those sex-crazed male students.'

The thought of those determined little hands sliding over another man's skin, setting another man's nerve endings on fire, had made his stomach muscles quiver in rejection.

'Sex crazed sounds interesting…' Poppy's delicious husky laugh had stopped as she studied his face. 'You're jealous!' The discovery had appeared to delight her.

'Heartless little witch,' he had condemned with a grin.

'*Your* heartless little witch, Luca,' she had reminded him quietly.

The undisguised love and confidence shining in the incredible eyes that had met his had made things tighten painfully in his chest. Poppy never tried to disguise anything. It had all been there on her face, in her voice, the expressive sweep of her slim hands—she was utterly and totally transparent.

Gianluca, the product of a calm home where voices were never raised in either anger or pleasure, where dignity and control were the order of the day, was less comfortable with spontaneous displays of emotion.

He was, to quote Poppy, 'a work in progress'.

'That makes a difference,' he had admitted huskily.

'Don't worry, Luca, I will tell all the sex-crazed students that my heart is taken by a computer geek.'

Her smile, never far away, had peeked out again like sun from behind a cloud as she had added, 'You do know I suppose that computer geeks are not meant to have muscles or look so hot? Though actually I think you'd look pretty good with glasses, sort of sexy intellectual...?' She had traced the shape of spectacles on his face with her finger and squinted at the imaginary outline. 'Yes, very Clark Kent.'

'You think I am a geek?'

'A hot geek. Oh, don't worry, there's no need to play it down, and don't deny it because I know you do. You don't have to be embarrassed or anything. I love it that you're super brainy. By the time I finish my degree you'll have created the most successful computer web-design company in the world,' she had predicted with a happy sigh. 'It's actually perfect timing.'

'How do you manage to be upbeat all the time?' And be so damned perceptive.

'It's all part of my charm and anyhow how could I not be upbeat? Everything is perfect except...' Tongue caught between her teeth, she had directed a stare of smouldering challenge at his face. 'You do know that this is the exact spot where we first kissed?'

'I have not forgotten. Stop that, Poppy,' he had warned, unable to take his eyes off her luscious mouth.

'Stop what, Luca?' Poppy had produced a look of mock innocence and patted the grass. 'Don't you think it would be kind of...appropriate if it was the same spot we...?'

Feeling noble and in extreme pain, he had clamped his hand over the slim dextrous fingers that were slipping the buttons on her blouse and, breathing hard through the fog of lust clouding his vision, dragged her to her feet, but not before it had become clear that Poppy was not wearing a bra.

Nobility was definitely overrated!

It was very hard to shield someone from your baser instincts when they didn't want to be protected. Promises to his godmother or not, had there not been an ice-cold loch for him to walk into fully clothed things might have turned out differently.

'I appreciate this, Dad, I really do, but actually it's a bit early.' And he had always seen Poppy wearing an emerald to match her eyes on her finger. 'And she's very young.'

And *very* impatient with his own reservations when it came to taking their relationship to the next level. The five-year age gap between them did not bother Poppy.

But it bothered him, and in deference to her inexperience from the beginning he had gone slow, keeping his lust under fierce control, not wanting to take advantage or scare her.

'The first time should be special,' he had shouted, standing waist deep in the water as he shook the water from his hair before slicking it back with a not quite steady hand.

'It won't be special if I die of old age waiting.'

'I promised your grandmother I wouldn't—'

'Break my heart, I know, but you're not going to and I'm eighteen, Luca, and I'm not going to change my mind. This isn't a crush—if it was I'd think you're perfect and I don't, but I love you despite your faults.'

Laughing, he had waded from the water. 'Please don't enumerate them…again—you're bad for my ego.'

'Your ego, Luca Ranieri, is bomb and bullet proof,' Poppy had contended lovingly.

'There's a beach in Southern Thailand.'

'Who did you see the beach with?'

'I was alone.'

Her furrowed brow had smoothed. 'Good.'

'You can only get to it by boat, the sand is white and the air is warm and when the moon is shining and the waves are lapping on the shore—'

'Stop!' Poppy had begged with a sigh. 'You had me at "there's". You could make a dictionary sound seductive when you use that voice, Luca Ranieri. Look,' she had instructed, rolling up her sleeve and extending a bare forearm towards him. 'I've got goose bumps…all over.' A wicked gleam had appeared in her eyes. 'Want to see?'

Luca had groaned. 'You know I do.'

'Except your old-fashioned sense of honour and a fear of Gran is stopping you,' she had completed fondly. 'Fine, have it your way. I'll let you woo me slowly, but don't expect me to stop trying,' she had warned him.

'Aurelia loves rubies.'

'Aurelia...' Luca closed the box with a click. 'I'm not marrying Aurelia.'

Both families had never made a secret of the wish that their two dynasties should be united by a marriage. As children he and Aurelia had frequently joked about their parents' old-fashioned, ambitious and ultimately unrealistic plans.

In recent years Aurelia who had gone the finishing-school route rather than university, had been around less to enjoy the joke on the rare occasions when the subject had been mentioned—less a plan now and more a wistful aspiration, or so it had seemed to Luca.

'I'm in love with someone else.' The truth seemed to him the simplest way to draw a line under the subject once and for all.

'Of course you're in love with someone else, Luca, you're twenty-three and I'm sure she's impossibly un-suitable.'

The patronising note in his father's voice set his teeth on edge.

'Do you realise how few women understand the responsibility that marrying into a family like ours brings?' Damiano said, warming to his theme. 'It's all about breeding. Girls today want their own careers—obviously your wife can never work.'

Despite the situation he had walked unwittingly into, the thought of Poppy's reaction if he told her he was about to chain her to the kitchen sink almost made Gianluca smile.

'They do not understand the concept of duty...the question is do you?' Damiano fired a fierce look at his son. 'And if we are talking love, what about Aurelia? She is in love with you and she has been waiting patiently.'

'That's rubbish!' Luca was horrified by the suggestion.

Seeing the flash of doubt in his son's eyes, Damiano arched a bushy brow. 'Is it? You have trained for your future career and she has trained for hers. Where is the problem—you like her...?'

'Liking is not enough.'

'Love again...' his father drawled impatiently. 'Do you think I was in love with your mother?'

'Yes.' Everyone knew his parents had made good of their marriage.

His father had the grace to look sheepish. 'Yes, well, that's not the point.'

'It isn't?'

'The point is you were always going to marry the girl, Luca, eventually. So why not now?'

Rather than dispute the false claim, Gianluca, sure he was missing something, addressed the question that puzzled him most. 'Why now? Why the sudden urgency?'

His father ducked the question.

'Oh, I know you had plans to travel or whatever.'

'When I agreed to the post-grad year at Harvard you knew I intended to take a gap year once I graduated with an MBA.'

'Like your friends…but you are not like your friends. You have already seen the world several times.'

'From the window of five-star hotels.'

'Yes, you have really suffered, Luca.'

'I know I have been fortunate.'

'You have been given everything and now it is time to give something back. It's time you remembered your duty to your family…your name…it's time you settled down, my boy.'

'The moral blackmail is not going to work this time.'

His father ignored the interruption. 'When you take over the company—'

'I am not going to take over the company.' Gianluca could still recall the relief he had felt having made the confession—it had been short-lived.

The anger died from his voice as his father sank heavily into a chair. 'If you don't marry Aurelia there will be no company for you to take over.'

'What are you talking about?'

Returning to the safe, his father came back with a file. 'You know the name Jason Stone?'

'Of course I do.' Everyone knew the name of the American who had given a new meaning to the word con.

Luca had always been mystified how the man who had nothing but charm to sell had had to fight off wealthy clients convinced by all his wild promises and eager to put their fortunes in his unscrupulous hands.

The man was now behind bars; of the missing billions there was no sign.

'Read it, Luca,' his father instructed.

As he scanned the pages he realised why his father was looking older…he suddenly felt older himself.

'How much?' he asked finally.

His father mentioned a figure that drew a groan from Gianluca.

'I thought it was safe and I thought I would be able to pay it back before anyone—'

'You used money from the...?' Gianluca, seeing his father's expression, bit back his reproach. 'Who knows?' Even the suggestion of embezzlement, when added to the disgrace of financial ruin on this scale, would be impossible to hide. 'Mother...?' Emotionally vulnerable, she worshipped her husband. The shame of such a scandal, Gianluca realised, would be hard if not impossible for her to bear.

'The bank, obviously, though not all, and Alessandro... he warned me at the time, but too late now.'

Mention of Aurelia's father made Gianluca stiffen, he knew what was coming.

'You know you are the son Alessandro never had and after his last heart attack he feels he needs to hand over the reins. He has run a deal past me...a form of merger. His offer is very generous, Luca, and it will all be kept within the family.'

And now they were family, Gianluca had stepped up to the mark and done what was expected of him—did that make him a hero or a coward?

Aware that such speculation was futile, he pushed away the question. His future was mapped out and he had no regrets, he told himself. He had done the right thing...the only thing.

Duty had been drummed into him since birth. He had made his choice and he would live with it. He would make his marriage work.

Next year Alessandro Cosimo would retire, his own father had already stepped down from his position as CEO, and Gianluca would take charge of the merged business empires.

He had hurt Poppy. It didn't matter how often he told himself she was young, she would get over it, move on, be happy with someone else…someone who wasn't him…the knowledge she was hurting because of him ate away at him like corrosive acid.

The thought of her being with someone else—this pain he locked away waiting until it would pass, because it would.

It had to!

She had come today. That he hadn't expected—why?

He'd never seen Poppy in heels before. The ones she wore today were high and spiky, the bare skin of her shapely calves a toasty pale gold. Attired in a silk shift a shade paler than her green eyes, she looked poised, effortlessly elegant and supremely desirable.

The service in the cathedral with a strategically placed marble column to hide behind had been the place to shed tears, or even during the speeches, but not out in the sunlit gardens while a lady in a very large hat was waiting for her to respond to a question.

Not now, thought Poppy as she took a deep breath and, ignoring her aching cheek muscles, produced an utterly fake smile of brilliant proportions as she snatched a glass from the tray of a passing waiter.

It was a struggle to swallow the fizzing liquid past the emotional lump that lay like a lead weight lodged behind her breastbone. She tossed it back in one deep swallow before excusing herself from large-hat lady in her halting Italian.

Luca had been teaching her, and, though each summer she had increased her vocabulary, her grammar was still shaky. He was a good teacher. Poppy had always planned that he teach her other things. Eyes scrunched closed, she shook her head, causing the dangling beaten-gold discs suspended from her ears to ring like bells as they brushed her neck.

God, she hated him!

She heard her grandmother call her name and pretended not to hear as she wound a hasty path between the guests who had spilled out onto the manicured lawns overlooking the hillsides covered in olive groves and topped with the darker green of pines.

She held back the tears until she reached the relative seclusion of a small gazebo hidden behind a hedge of tall fragrant lavender.

How had this happened? Life had been perfect and now…had Luca fallen out of love with her? In her head she could hear his voice telling her that it had been a mistake.

Had he ever loved her?

Did he love the perfect Aurelia?

What was not to love? she thought darkly, seeing the tall raven-haired beauty standing at his side and feeling the familiar knife thrust of jealousy. Aurelia didn't have a mother who made the cover of every European scandal sheet on a monthly basis!

Shaking her head to stem the constant flow of tortured thoughts, Poppy reached into her bag for the wad of tissues inside.

'Damn!' She sniffed as they fell to the floor. Bending to pick them up, she froze.

And then he was there, she could feel him.

Poppy lifted her head and he just stood there. Even though he was twenty feet away she could feel the emotion coming off him in waves as he walked towards her.

'You're crying.'

Poppy scrunched the tissues in her hand and got to her feet. 'No—hay fever,' she lied.

'Why did you come, Poppy?'

'I didn't believe you'd really do it...but you did. Wow, you really did... Did you mean any of it, Luca? Or was it just some sort of sick game?'

His hand extended then dropped to his side. 'You feel bad now, Poppy, but you'll forget—'

'I don't want to forget.' She gave a sniff and managed a watery smile. 'I hope you'll both be very happy.'

His jaw clenched as his eyes fell from hers.

'I meant it. I meant everything.' The words seemed wrenched from his throat against his will.

Seeing the pain in his eyes, Poppy told herself she was *glad* he was suffering. He deserved to suffer—this was his doing. So why did she want to run to his side and hug him?

'And that makes it better how?' Poppy tried to make her voice cold but it quivered pathetically.

She watched his expression grow blank until the muscle clenching in his jaw was the only visible evidence of emotion.

'Why, Luca? Why have you done this?'

'Things...' He dragged a hand through his dark hair. 'It is complicated.'

'Do you love her...?' She let out a soft wail and, teeth

gritted, covered her ears with her hands. 'No, don't tell me. I don't want to know and don't you dare feel sorry for me,' she hissed fiercely.

Luca took her face between his hands and looked down into her tragic tear-stained face. 'Have a great life, Poppy,' he said, kissing her lips gently before he turned and walked away.

CHAPTER ONE

Poppy left her overnight bag in the hallway and walked into the dining room of her parents' garden flat. The remains of breakfast still on the table, her father was working his way through a stack of Sunday newspapers and her stepmother's fingers were flying with the nimble precision Poppy always envied across the current tapestry she was working on while chuckling at the programme she was listening to on the radio.

The comforting familiarity of the domestic scene smoothed the furrow etched in Poppy's smooth brow. It hadn't always been this way. Until the arrival of Millie on the scene Sundays, and for that matter every other day in the Ramsay household, had been very different. At ten Poppy had not realised some fathers did not spend the entire weekend at the office. Millie, she reflected fondly, had changed their lives utterly and very much for the better—it was just a shame that her grandmother still refused to recognise this.

Millie Ramsay glanced up, the smile of welcome on her pretty freckled face fading into a look of concern as she took in her stepdaughter's troubled expression. 'A problem, Poppy?' she asked, laying aside her work.

'Yes,' Poppy admitted, perching on the arm of her

father's chair as he laid down his newspaper with a rustle. She paused and shot an apologetic look Millie's way before responding.

'It's Gran,' she said, thinking, *Cue awkward silence.*

Robert Ramsay's expression had iced over before his newspaper came up with a rustle. Millie, her serenity unruffled, switched off the laughter on the radio.

It was Millie who broke the growing awkward silence.

'Is your grandmother not well, Poppy?' she asked, getting to her feet.

Behind his newspaper her husband cleared his throat noisily. Millie sighed at the strangled sound as she said quietly, 'She's an old lady, and she's your mother, Rob.'

A second snort then silence from behind the newspaper greeted this quiet reproach.

'She's fine—well, not ill at least,' Poppy said, addressing her response to Millie. 'On Thursday when we spoke on the phone, I could tell from her voice something was wrong.' After a lot of probing the truth had finally emerged. 'It turns out she'd had a letter from the council that had upset her—not the first.' When pressed her grandmother had admitted the rather one-sided dialogue with the local authority had been going on for nine months.

'And let me guess…Mother ignored them?'

'It looks like it,' Poppy said, addressing her reply to the newspaper. 'It started when a hiker using the public footpath—the one that goes through the kitchen garden—broke his ankle. He complained and from what I can gather it seems someone came out to investigate and…well, the outcome was they discovered the entire west wall of the east wing is in danger of falling down.'

Robert Ramsay's newspaper came down. 'The west wall has been falling down since I was a boy,' he said scornfully. 'The entire place has been falling down, but I don't see what business that is of the council or, for that matter, anyone else.'

'Pretty much Gran's reaction, but Inverannoch Castle is a listed building, Dad, and as the owner Gran is legally responsible for maintaining the fabric of the building.' A brief Internet search had revealed that much. 'And as the footpath runs so close it becomes a health and safety issue...'

'Health and safety!' Her father snorted. 'A load of mollycoddling rubbish!'

'Again pretty much Gran's response, once she stopped throwing the letters from the council's legal department on the fire. Reading between the lines, I got the impression she's managed to offend just about everybody and now, well...' The furrow between Poppy's dark feathery brows deepened. 'She's really afraid she could lose Inverannoch, and I think she might be right.'

'Oh, dear!' Millie said, glancing towards her husband, who had hidden again behind his newspaper. 'What do you think, Rob?'

'It's a fuss about nothing.'

'I hope so,' Poppy said quietly.

'Ring the council if you're worried.'

'I did, I spent half of Friday being put on hold. But they wouldn't discuss it with me, which is why I've decided to go up there and find out for myself.'

'What?' Robert Ramsays's incredulous deep voice boomed. His paper came down with a rustle. 'You're not serious?'

Poppy lifted her chin. 'I'm on my way to the airport,

Dad. I just dropped by to tell you. I'll ring when I arrive in Inverness. I'll hire a car there.'

'Drop everything and hare off to the back of beyond just because of a letter!' Robert Ramsay rolled his eyes contemptuously. 'Talk about overreaction. If you expect your grandmother to be grateful for this dramatic gesture...'

'I don't,' Poppy admitted, a brief grin momentarily lighting the sombre cast of her features. 'She'll tell me I'm interfering and that she's more than capable of sorting out her own affairs.' Her smile faded. 'Aren't you even a little bit concerned, Dad?'

Her father's eyes fell. 'If you're really *that* worried,' he grunted, 'give her the number of my solicitors, but I think you'll find it is all a storm in a teacup.'

'I really hope you're right and it's a wasted journey, Dad, but I am going.'

Robert Ramsay eyed the stubborn set of his daughter's jaw and shook his head. 'You always were an obstinate child.'

'I can't imagine where I got that from.'

Poppy watched her father fight a smile. 'All right, if you won't listen to me what about this boyfriend of yours? What does *he* think of you dashing off this way? And what about work? I thought you'd used up your annual leave.'

Not the *ideal* moment she had been waiting for, but... Poppy took a deep breath. 'I don't have a boyfriend, and I handed in my notice last month.'

Taking advantage of the stunned silence that followed her casual disclosure, Poppy made a hasty exit turning a deaf ear and closing the door on her father's bellow.

* * *

Adrenaline still surging through his bloodstream, Gianluca, his chest heaving from the exertion of the swim to shore, dragged a hand over the salty water streaming down his face and watched for a moment as the boat he had owned for almost an hour—not his best financial investment—smashed itself to matchwood on the rocks, before turning his back on the scene of devastation.

The ten-mile track around the mist-shrouded mountain in a gale would, it turned out, even allowing for recent rock slides that had apparently washed away part of the track, have been the safer choice, but then hindsight was a marvellous thing.

The warnings of the locals that he had listened politely to before choosing to ignore them had clearly not been exaggerated, unlike the price he had paid for the vessel.

The guy who sold it to him had had no qualms when it came to fleecing a stranger—on another occasion Gianluca might even have admired his enterprise.

He shrugged, his firm lips twitching upwards at the corners into an ironic smile that faded as his lean body was shaken by a deep tremor and then another. He clenched his jaw and blinked away the water that still streamed steadily into his eyes and assessed his situation.

A man did not have to be a survival expert to work out standing here second-guessing his choices was not a good idea. The exposed pebbly beach offered zero shelter from the wind that cut through the wet clothes he wore like a cold surgical blade sending the chill of his skin bone deep, and blue had never really been his colour, he thought, grimacing as he rubbed the skin of his forearms to kick-start the circulation.

Standing here inviting hypothermia would only confirm the locals' opinion that he was an idiot. According to them taking the small boat out in the storm had been inviting worse than hypothermia and as it turned out they had very nearly been right. Not that Gianluca, who possessed a pragmatic attitude to such things, wasted more than a moment contemplating how close he had come to a fate similar to that of the vessel.

He had chosen to take a calculated risk, something he had done before, though admittedly his own skin was not generally at risk, and in this instance the risk had not been *entirely* successful. On the plus side, he might be temporarily stranded but he had reached his goal.

He turned his back on the cauldron of grey foaming waves and directed his narrowed gaze speculatively towards the outline of Inverannoch Castle visible through the mist.

The turreted stone building, even in its present semi-derelict state, was imposing—in a grim and forbidding sort of way. Much, he mused, like the old lady who lived there, his godmother Isabel Ramsay.

He had been attending an international conference in Edinburgh where he had been guest speaker when he had received a phone call from his very anxious grandmother, who was worried after speaking to her old friend Isabel.

'She's putting a brave face on it, Gianluca, but she's really upset, I could tell, and that's just not like Isabel. Do you really think she could lose the castle? You won't let it happen, will you?'

It would have been hard to fulfil his promise if he had gone down with his ship, he mused as he strode towards the steps cut in the stone cliff past what remained of an old harbour wall, a reminder of the glory days when the castle had been the destination of the rich and glamorous of the day. Possessing the balance of a natural athlete and a lean, toned body to match it, he did not slow as he negotiated the lethally slippery worn steps.

From the top of the cliff the castle, hidden by a forested area, was no longer visible. Someone who was not familiar with the area would not have seen the path through the trees. It took Gianluca a few moments to locate it. Years ago he had been as familiar with every track as he was with his own hand. Now…in recent years his visits to the castle had been to see his godmother and had not involved reacquainting himself with the landscape.

Unsure of his welcome, he had come back that first time eighteen months after his wedding. Since then a sense of duty had made him undertake the painful trip once or twice a year. Seven years now, he made the calculation with a sense of shock, but the visits were rarely more than fleeting overnight stopovers, the private helicopter either waiting for him or returning the next morning to pick him up.

A loud crack broke into his private reflections and Gianluca instinctively stepped back, narrowly avoiding the large branch that fell at his feet—no surprise there had been no pilot willing or suicidal enough to bring him out here today!

He had always supposed that it would have got easier over the years, but no—the place just held too many memories… He had judged it best to limit his contact and avoid falling into the trap of indulging in the sort of sentimental nostalgia that he despised.

Considering his reluctance to spend more than a night here, he had been surprised by how strongly he had reacted to the idea of the resident Ramsay being forced from her home and the crumbling castle being restored by others, not as a home, but a destination on a tourist map.

How would Poppy react if her grandmother was forced from her home?

He pushed the thought away—the past belonged in the past—and walked towards the densely packed trees that offered some shelter from the wind. They also reduced the daylight, such as it was that remained. Wishing he had had the forethought to grab a torch before he had abandoned the boat to its fate, he added a few scratches from overhanging branches to the bruises he could not yet feel. That was something to look forward to when he thawed out.

From this side of the trees he saw what had not been visible from the shore: the lights shining from the windows of the inhabited rooms in the west wing.

CHAPTER TWO

POPPY having finally managed to fan the flames of the open fire in the cavernous fireplace into life, had peeled off her gloves—she had no intention of relinquishing her padded jacket—and was warming her fingers by the flickering flames when the sound of the brass door knocker hitting the oak door once, twice and then again made her fall back on her heels. Eyes on the door, she scrambled to her feet, rubbing her hands on the seat of her pants.

On finding the place deserted when she had arrived earlier, she had frantically searched the castle from top to bottom, her hunt extending outside until the weather had closed in and forced her to retreat.

Was this the rescue party she had been praying for?

Or better still was it Gran herself who would stroll in and demand to know what all the fuss was about?

Had her grandmother been out there all along? It would be just like her not to allow the elements to interfere with her daily constitutional.

'Gran?' Heart thudding hopefully, she left the warmth of the fire. Even though Poppy hadn't bolted the massive metal-banded oak door or turned the big old-fashioned key in the lock—there hadn't seemed any point—it seemed to take her an age to manipulate the latch and open the door.

The door swung inwards painfully slowly, then, caught by a gust of wind, almost knocked her over before it hit the stone wall with a tremendous crash to reveal, not her grandmother, but the tall sinister outline of a man—a large man.

It was a situation where an active imagination became a curse and Poppy's immediately went into overdrive. She flinched and sucked in a deep breath as the tall figure was suddenly backlit by a flash of lightning that illuminated the sky for a brief moment.

A scream locked in her throat, Poppy stood there nailed to the spot by a stab of visceral fear while her heart tried to batter its way out of her chest and a bass toll of thunder cracked in perfect horror movie tradition overhead.

The scream emerged as a choked gasp when the figure, without saying a word, took a step forward. Jolted free of the fear-induced paralysis that had gripped her, Poppy shadowed the step hastily retreating, one hand pressed to her throat, before she turned and ran back to the fireplace.

She lifted the heavy poker that lay there. It took both hands to raise it and she whirled back to face the intruder warning fiercely, 'I'm not alone!' The normally husky timbre of her voice became shrill as she warned darkly, 'It's true!'

Not the best of time to discover that the people who had claimed she couldn't lie convincingly if her life depended on it were right.

'I'm glad to hear it.' Gianluca scanned the room. Of his godmother there was no immediate sign, just the weapon-wielding figure in a thick padded jacket. His glance moved to the face framed by a knitted hat complete with furry earflaps.

The resulting jolt of recognition sent a pulse of shock zigzagging through his body with the strength of a lightning bolt. The last time he had looked directly at those spectacular, exotically slanted green eyes they had been filled with sad tears.

It was an image he had spent years trying to bury.

'And don't think I'm afraid to use this because I'm not—' She stopped abruptly, her eyes widening…that voice…deep with the faint foreign inflection…no. Her heartbeat rocketed and her stomach dropped into a big black hole.

Calm down, Poppy, she counselled herself. *You're imagining things. It can't be… Could it?*

Still brandishing her weapon, she tilted her head back, directing a wary look at the intruder's face. The furrow in her brow deepened and her arms began to ache with the effort of maintaining her defensive pose as she struggled in the gloom to see the man's face.

Frustratingly all she could make out was an undefined blur and the impression of strong angles, sharp planes and dramatic hollows. Then the figure, not apparently deterred by her threats, stepped forward into a convenient pool of candlelight.

Poppy shook her head in a negative motion, intensifying the dizzy sensation.

'No! You can't be here.' She began to cough as the candle on the table beside her guttered, sending up a plume of acrid smoke. *'Luca?'*

As if there could be two men that looked like this!

Poppy had no doubt that one day she would be able

to look back on the last occasion they had spoken and not feel physically sick, but seven years and that day had definitely not come!

Heart pounding—was she going to have a heart attack?—she slowly laid the heavy poker down onto the hearth and tried frantically to marshal her rioting thoughts as she watched Luca brace his shoulder against the door and push. The wind and ancient wood resisted his efforts until, angular jaw clenched, the sinews in his brown neck standing out, with a final grunt of effort he managed to force the door that had been built to hold back armies closed with a loud bang.

The noise of the storm raging outside immediately lowered by several decibels. It was quiet enough now for Poppy to hear the click of the grandfather clock and the steady drip of the water gathering in a pool on the stone flagstones around the feet of Gianluca Ranieri.

She was here *alone* with Luca. Somewhere in her chest a bubble of terror burst... *I can't do this!* Poppy yanked herself back from the brink of outright panic and hid her confused feelings behind a tight controlled smile.

'I barely recognised you,' she lied, averting her gaze from the perfect symmetry of a bronzed face bisected by a masterful nose and slashing cheekbones. 'You've changed, Luca.'

This at least was not a lie. He was still the best-looking man imaginable—it was really nice to be able to make the observation with total objectivity, not soppy, misty-eyed foolishness, but the aura of power that hung around him like a second skin made him seem more aloof. And his heavy-lidded eyes, dark and fringed by incredibly long, spiky lashes—they had not in the past held a cynical gleam that suggested their owner expected the worst from the world and was rarely disappointed.

'You haven't.' It was hard to tell from his abrupt delivery if this was a criticism or a compliment. 'I did not expect you to be here.'

He didn't add *or wild horses would not have dragged me here* to his vaguely accusatory statement, but he didn't have to. He looked about as happy to see her as he had two years earlier, the night she had almost literally bumped into him as she was emerging with a group of friends from a popular West End show.

He had cut her dead.

Poppy had been left standing on the pavement, the awkward half-smile of polite acknowledgement still on her face. The public slight had not gone unnoticed.

'Someone you know?' one of the men in the group had asked.

Poppy had shrugged off the hurt inflicted by the chilling indifference in the dark eyes that had moved with the barest hint of recognition over her face.

'Not really.'

Shaking some of the excess moisture from his hair, Luca moved forward into the room. Poppy responded with several backwards steps, reminding him of a jittery thoroughbred.

'I am not, to my knowledge, infectious.'

She had no smart response to the mild sarcasm and no easy answer for why she felt the need to keep him at several arms' lengths.

'This is…' she expelled a gusty sigh, her expression reflecting her dismay, and tore off her cap, tossing it on top of a pile of newspapers on a nearby armchair '…a total nightmare.' There seemed very little point putting a brave face on what was an awful situation. A dangerous stranger she could have legitimately clonked on the head with a poker...what was she meant to do with Luca?

Her glance slid to the stern outline of his beautiful—it really was—mouth... A tiny sigh escaped her parted lips. She had once had a lot of ideas about what to do with and to Luca, but few, actually none, were any longer appropriate.

He tilted his head in acknowledgement. 'The storm is bad.'

Poppy gave herself a mental shake and let his misinterpretation remain uncorrected as she struggled to make her fuzzy brain work... How...why was Luca here? 'Was Gran expecting you?'

'No.'

Gianluca's eyes followed the golden brown waves as they continued to bounce, settling in a silky messy halo around her shoulders. It slid down her back, falling below shoulder-blade level, longer than she had used to wear it. The shaggy fringe was gone too, revealing the purity of her delicate heart-shaped face. A face still dominated, but not overwhelmed, by slanted hazel-green eyes.

'So you don't know where she is?' Poppy pressed.

The furrow between his brows deepened as he registered the anxiety behind her question. 'Don't you?' He struggled to focus on the situation and not on every tiny detail of her face.

Poppy bit her lip and shook her head. 'I've looked everywhere and there's no sign of her.' She had scoured the surrounding area yelling until her throat was raw.

'Did you look for a note?'

His glance moved in an assessing sweep around the rapidly darkening room that, though not in the grand part of the building, still had twice the square footage of an average semi.

'Of course I looked for a note.'

'I'm assuming the candles are not for atmosphere.' Even as he spoke Luca realised that it was a mistake to assume anything; for all he knew Poppy might be here with a boyfriend. 'The power's out?' On every visit he suggested that the electrics needed an overhaul; his suggestion was inevitably met with a point-blank refusal from his frugal godmother, who was fond of saying she did not believe in change for change's sake.

Poppy nodded and glanced at her watch, her eyes widening when she read the time. 'Nearly two hours ago.' Just after she had arrived.

'Did you check the fuses?'

There was an edge in her voice as Poppy replied, 'Of course I checked the fuses.'

'Isn't there still a back-up generator?'

Poppy struggled against impatience. 'Yes, but it's not working.'

He arched a brow. 'And you know this how?'

'I tried to start it.' Though it was notoriously temperamental, the second kick generally did the trick, but not today.

She saw something flicker at the back of his dark eyes. 'You kicked it?'

Poppy killed the beginning of a grin that tugged at the corners of her mouth and experienced a moment of panic before her instincts of self-preservation kicked in. It had taken her a very long time to put the memories they shared into cold storage; she wasn't about to thaw out even at the most innocent of them, not now, not ever.

'As a last resort.'

Frustrated in his attempts to read past her cool mask, he felt a stab of dissatisfaction. She might have changed remarkably little to look at—Poppy could still have passed for a teenager—but clearly she had changed.

And you expected she wouldn't, Luca? You expected that having her heart broken would not have made her toughen up, develop a few defences?

'And Isabel, you saw her last...*when*?'

Poppy responded to the question literally. 'April.'

His dark brows drew together above the bridge of his hawkish nose. 'I meant...'

Intercepting the impatient look, she flushed and, resenting the fact he had made her feel foolish, inserted quickly, 'I know what you meant, and, no, I haven't seen Gran, but I spoke to her...last night.' Had it really only been a few hours earlier?

'This isn't a case of miscommunication—perhaps she went to the village to meet you?'

'No, I said I'd catch the ferry and I'd ring when I arrived.'

'There was no reply?'

'The phone lines are down and I couldn't get a signal on my mobile. Where can she be, Luca? The only way out of here is by boat, and don't,' she pleaded, 'suggest she might have walked out, because after the rock fall last winter even a four-wheel drive can't make it up the track.'

'I was not going to suggest she walked out. Your

gran's fit for an eighty-year-old but even she is not going to trek out along the mountain track.'

'I have a *bad* feeling, Luca.' It was just a name and what was she meant to call him—Mr Ranieri? 'Admittedly my *feelings* are not infallible.'

Her *feelings* about Luca had been all good, they had told her that Luca was the one, that he was totally trustworthy. Annoyed with herself for allowing ancient history to divert her, Poppy gave her head a tiny negative shake of irritation. She should be focusing on Gran. She *was*, and realistically she couldn't exactly ignore Luca, she just had to keep her response…proportionate.

'There's probably a simple explanation.'

'Like Gran is lying out there hurt, unable to call for help…or worse? That sort of simple?' She swallowed and pushed away the image and sucked in a steadying breath through flared nostrils. 'Maybe I am overthinking it…? Maybe there is a simple explanation?' She shot him a look of appeal, willing him to convince her.

Luca did not offer comfort and support, but then it wasn't his job. Instead he gave a non-committal grunt. 'I am assuming you are here because of the issue with the council?'

Her emerald eyes flew to his face, wide with surprise. '*You* know about that? Gran asked for your help?' Of course she had.

And why not?

It was utterly insane to feel a sense of betrayal—there was no reason that Gran shouldn't turn to Luca. He was her godson. Poppy knew they still had contact and she was fine with that; she didn't want to know the details, but she was fine with it—*totally*.

Her gran appreciated she didn't want to know about

Luca's life—hard not to after her response to a conversation that had opened with, 'When Luca was here last month...'

Up until that memorable moment—memorable for all the wrong reasons—Poppy had considered herself totally over it...him... It turned out that eighteen months hadn't been long enough.

Luca tipped his dark head in acknowledgement. 'The bare bones, no details—my grandmother contacted me. She was concerned.'

Poppy's tense expression was momentarily lightened as an image of a slight figure who still retained a strong Highland accent even though she had lived the last fifty years of her life in Italy flashed into her head.

'Aunt Fiona?' The title was honorary, the only connection being a friendship between the older women that had survived despite the disparate paths their lives had taken since their schooldays. 'How is she?'

'Well.'

His eyes drifted slowly over the smooth curve of her cheeks; reaching the full curve of her lush wide mouth, he had zero control over the lustful reaction of his body.

'She was always k-kind to me.'

The kindness had been a stark contrast to the attitude of his parents, who had acted as though she had a contagious disease when she had attended a birthday tea in a posh London hotel for Luca's grandmother.

It had been Luca who found her crying in the cloakroom.

'So my mum gets married a lot and is sometimes photographed without many clothes—she's never killed anyone! I think your family are mean and horrible!'

'Did I ever tell you about the time that my mum

came out of the ladies' room with her skirt tucked into her knickers? Or the dinner where my father thought the host was the wine waiter and told him the wine was corked?'

He had continued to tell her scandalous and probably untrue stories that made his parents look ridiculous until she had laughed.

'Poppy...?' Concern roughened the edges of his velvet voice.

Poppy's eyes lifted. She blinked twice to clear her swimming vision and reminded herself she was a competent twenty-first-century woman, not some wimpy heroine in a Victorian melodrama, and even if she had needed a masculine chest to bury her face in Luca's was already spoken for.

'This doesn't look good, does it?' she said, directing a 'give it to me straight I can take it' look at his dark lean face.

She could hide a lot, but not the fear in her luminous eyes. Gianluca studied the emerald stare directed his way and felt something twist hard in his gut.

'Do not jump to conclusions,' he cautioned. 'You always did have a tendency to be over-emotional.' And outspoken, sentimental, not to mention extremely stubborn, but most of all Poppy had always been herself more so than any person he had ever met.

'We all move on, Luca.' She didn't bother trying to make the message subtle. 'But cross my heart I'll do my level best not to have hysterics,' she promised. 'So what next?'

'Next I dry off.'

'You're wet...?' As Poppy made the belated observation her gaze travelled upwards from his feet. *Hard...*

the word popped into her head and stayed there; grey-hound lean and tough, there was no vestige of anything approaching softness in Luca.

'Top marks for observation.'

Poppy dragged her eyes to his face. 'But what I don't understand... How did you get out here, with the storm...?' Her voice trailed away as her glance shifted to the mullioned window that was being battered by a shower of freakishly large hailstones.

The ferry wasn't running and the only person willing to ferry her here from Ullapool had refused to wait a moment after she disembarked, so anxious—with good reason as it turned out—had he been not to get caught out in open sea when the storm hit.

'I bought a boat.'

Poppy stared. He said it the same way someone might say, 'I bought a bar of chocolate.' He obviously didn't have a clue that he had said anything out of the ordinary.

'Of course you did.'

There were plus sides to his extravagance: at least they were no longer stranded when the storm abated; at least they had an exit route that did not involve SOS signals or swimming.

'I can't believe you made it here in this,' she mused, watching, her stomach performing helpless flips of appreciation, as he walked long-legged and effortlessly elegant like some jungle cat towards the fire.

'I did. The boat didn't.'

Poppy, her thoughts still very much involved with thoughts of his feral grace, was still joining the mental dots when he added, 'It sank.'

CHAPTER THREE

'SANK!' The images crowding into her head made her feel physically sick.

As Poppy estimated her chances of getting to the bathroom before she threw up Luca calmly threw a log on the smouldering fire and tossed an almost absent look over his shoulder before he reached for the poker she had dropped.

'Not my finest moment. I *almost* made it.' The *almost* continued to irritate. 'But the undertow and the rocks...' He shrugged his magnificent shoulders and began to prod the reluctant flames.

She regarded him incredulously. Could anyone sane be this casual about a near-death experience?

'The boat smashed on the rocks?' she said tightly.

He nodded.

'You could have drowned.' And Luca was acting as if the possibility had not even occurred to him. Her indignation grew. It was nothing to her if he decided to kill himself but he had a wife and family responsibilities.

And I once found his reckless streak exciting!

It was reassuring to recognise how much she had changed. There was nothing *exciting* about the graphic images playing in her head that involved the grey waves closing over a dark head, sucking him down.

The look Luca slung over his shoulder was tinged with impatience. 'But I did not.' It was not his habit to expend energy on *what if* scenarios, in theory at least.

There were exceptions to this rule.

What if he had not chosen duty ahead of personal happiness? What if he hadn't caved into parental pressure? Seven years and that question had never completely gone away.

He accepted that no choice came without a price, what he could not accept or forgive himself for was others paying the price for his choices.

And for what?

He had kept the family name clear of scandal, he had discovered a talent for making money and found out that he did not have a talent for being a husband.

If he had learnt anything he now knew that marriage was not for him—he was simply not husband material; he was never again going to take on the responsibility for another human being's happiness.

Poppy, though she hadn't known it at the time, had actually had a lucky escape.

His meditative stare lingered on her face. And now here she was, in this place where they had met, and he was free. Was Poppy alone or in a relationship...maybe long term—the man he had seen her emerge from the theatre with? His eyes brushed her bare fingers—or maybe it was all new and exciting with a new lover?

'I am a very good swimmer.'

Poppy's eyes glazed when without warning his words caused a less traumatic but equally disturbing picture to form in her head—Luca, his sleek brown streamlined body cutting through the blue water before he stopped and, treading water, gestured for her to join him.

She rejected the random memory the same way she had rejected his invitation.

He had nearly died and he was acting as if it didn't matter. Was he too cool to care or just plain stupid?

'You know I feel sorry for the people that care about you.' Her eyes flashed wide as a previously unconsidered possibility occurred to her. 'I'm assuming that you were alone in the boat?'

'I'm alone and, as you see, alive.'

Her nose wrinkled. 'Barely.' Actually despite his brush with death, or maybe because of it, Luca radiated an aura of restless vitality.

His edgy glance slid her way. 'Can we end the post-mortem?' That she considered it possible that he'd leave a fellow traveller to their watery fate while he made himself comfortable spoke volumes on her opinion of him. 'Though obviously it's good to know someone cares.'

Missing entirely the sarcasm in his voice, Poppy tightened her soft lips as she injected a note of studied boredom into her voice and drawled, 'Been there done that.' Spurred by the flash of reaction she glimpsed in his dramatically dark eyes, she added with a smile that left her own eyes cold, 'So don't worry, Luca, you're safe. I won't be trying to seduce you any time soon.'

His dark lashes swept downwards then lifted. Two thirds of his brain knew it was a bad thing to say but the reckless, self-indulgent last third—blame it on a near-death experience—appeared to have temporary control of his vocal chords as he slurred. 'Am I meant to think that's a good thing?'

Poppy met his eyes, saw the dark dangerous un-spoken message, sensed the tension rolling off him in waves and felt her insides dissolve.

After several breathless seconds of mind-numbing, heart-racing excitement the shame and disgust kicked in.

What are you doing, Poppy? He's a married man who broke your heart! And if that made her bad it made him a total sleaze.

Poppy folded her arms across her chest. 'I'm sure your wife will be pleased you're alive.'

Message received, she thought, watching his expression blank. He did not look guilty, he looked… She shivered. The eyes that met hers had a flat, almost dead look.

Was his marriage in trouble…?

Not my business.

Admittedly once the possibility would have given her some feeling of shameful satisfaction. Happily she was no longer so bitter and twisted. She hadn't got noble suddenly, but she had wised up enough to know that one criteria of having a life was letting go of the bad stuff that happened.

Luca constituted bad stuff.

Bad but beautiful, she thought, studying his profile, but she was totally over him. The fact she felt the need to constantly remind herself of this was in itself a cause of concern.

'And you?' Back now turned to her, he draped his jacket with what seemed like elaborate care over the back of a wooden rocking chair before taking the hem of his drenched cashmere sweater and peeling it over his head.

'I am assuming you had a less eventful journey…?' He lifted an arm, pressing his hand to the back of his head as he rotated his neck and flexed his shoulders, causing the muscles of his powerful shoulders and upper arms to bunch and ripple in a manner that Poppy found very distracting.

Distracting might well be the understatement of the century!

'I had…' Poppy swallowed and struggled to focus on the question… *What was the question?*

Gianluca's torso was lean and tautly muscled; the drift of dark hair across his chest covered smooth bronze flesh that was tinged with blue and the surface studded with a rash of goose bumps. There was a livid-looking graze along his ribs and a discoloured area that looked like the beginning of a bruise.

The evidence of what had to be painful injuries made her sensitive stomach muscles spasm… Uncomfortably aware that empathy wasn't the only cause of the growing tension in her belly, Poppy closed her eyes for a moment to shut out all that disturbing rampant maleness, and cleared her throat.

'Much less eventful,' she explained to a point somewhere over Gianluca's left shoulder and continued to studiedly ignore the fact that despite the cold she was suddenly very hot in places that she ought not to be hot. 'I hired someone to ferry me out. Unfortunately he wouldn't hang around to wait for me for any money. What are you doing?' she added, her voice sharpening in alarm.

'Taking off my pants. It used, as I recall, to be your ambition.'

Poppy laughed, trying to match his flippancy. 'I'm

touched you remember. Imagine my surprise when I discovered that most men don't put up a fight.'

Before she could begin to question the flash of coruscating anger that lit up his dark eyes there was a deafening crack followed by a loud roar and a succession of bangs that made Poppy cover her ears with her hands and close her eyes.

Utterly convinced that the roof was falling in, she thought, God, the men in suits at the council were right!

Fatalistically prepared for what was to come, she held her breath and waited to feel the weight of the building come crashing down on her head. Instead she felt the pressure of two heavy hands on her hunched shoulders.

'You can breathe now.'

Poppy's eyes blinked open. Luca had moved in to stand directly in front of her. He was inches away, very solid and reassuring. 'What happened?'

'Not totally sure,' Luca admitted. 'But it was dramatic.' His dark head tipped in acknowledgement of the drama as he took hold of both her wrists and firmly removed her hands from her ears.

She glanced up nervously at the heavily beamed ceiling. There were no gaping holes. It actually looked reassuringly sturdy. 'I thought the roof was coming off,' she disclosed huskily.

'And you thought the best defence was to go into see-no-evil-hear-no-evil mode. Your survival instincts definitely need some work, *cara*!'

The killer combination of his throaty sexy voice and the casual endearment caused a black hole to open up without warning where her stomach had been.

'We can't all be ice cool in the face of danger.' She must have looked like a total fool but on the plus side she was not lying crushed under a pile of rubble. 'I didn't think,' she admitted huskily. 'I just sort of…reacted.'

Her heart thudding louder than it had been when she had thought she was about to be buried under several tons of rubble, Poppy's eyes flickered nervously towards the cool brown fingers circling her wrists. She ran the tip of her tongue across her dry lips; she was trying hard not to *react* now.

Reacting to her instincts at this moment would have involved snatching her hands from his grasp, an action he might well read too much into…or *maybe not*.

Luckily Gianluca remained oblivious to the uncomfortable things the light contact was doing to her. He wasn't even looking at her any longer, he was checking out the room, but he was still holding her wrists.

She gave a gentle tug but instead of responding to the reminder in the way he was meant to Gianluca tightened his grip and his thumbs began to move in circular sweeps over the blue-veined inner aspect of her wrists. Presumably meant to be soothing, the effect of the light pressure was however anything but.

Oh, help!

If she had found the contact disturbing this fresh assault on her senses was almost painful in its intensity. Previously her discomfort had taken the form of vague unease, a prickle under her skin and an empty feeling in her stomach. Now the tingle was a throb and the empty feeling a clenched fist of awareness.

This had to be some post-being-scared-half-to-death-on-top-of-a-very-bad-day scenario. The alternative was not good news.

Gianluca's attention shifted from the broken glass on the floor to the woman beside him. 'You're shaking.'

His concern took the form of a stern frown as his critical scrutiny moved across the soft contours of the heart shaped face turned up to him. Her skin was as pale as milk, making the purplish smudges under her eyes appear even darker. Her dark lashes lowered but not before he had taken note of the glow in those arresting eyes. It had a feverish quality.

'Are you running a temperature?' He had intended to lay his hand on her forehead to test his theory when something bright caught his eye.

'No, don't move,' he rebuked sharply as she shied away from his hand. 'There's a...' He pushed aside a section of shiny soft hair from her forehead—actually *very* soft—to grasp the slim sharp piece of glass that had enmeshed itself in her hair.

Poppy stopped breathing as his brown fingertips touched her skin, slivers of hot heat slid through her body.

'There, got it.' He held up the shard for her to see.

The thought of that wicked splinter piercing the skin of her face or neck made the muscles deep in his belly tighten.

'Thank you,' she murmured breathlessly.

'Come closer to the fire. You're still shaking.'

She was standing extremely close to a bare-chested virile man with the sort of delicious hard body that lustful fantasies were made of, shaking!

It was a relief to realise she was not drooling! Sexual attraction was not, she knew because she'd read the relevant articles, something a person could rationalise. Or, as she knew only too well, something a person could conjure up. She had tried and failed on more than one occasion.

'Of course I am. It's called shock.' This time when she tugged her wrists he let go; her reaction to freedom was worryingly ambivalent.

'Something just went bang.' Arms crossed over her chest, she rubbed her upper arms briskly and gave a rueful laugh adding, *'Loudly.'*

At that point it went bang again.

Poppy closed her eyes again but this time instinct did not lead her to cover her ears but step forward with a gasp into the hard male body positioned conveniently close.

Gianluca's arms folded around her as his big body curved protectively over her. A hand in the small of her back, he dragged her in closer. Head buried against his bare chest, she burrowed into him, her hands flat against his muscle-ridged belly. She could hear the thud of his heart as he cradled her and feel the coolness of his skin even through the layers of clothing she wore.

The noise stopped, but his arms did not fall away. When she looked back on the incident later Poppy had no idea how long they had stood there.

She did remember feeling strangely bereft when he released her.

Robbed of the intimate contact, her body continued to tingle as he stared at her, a frown between his dark slanting brows. She couldn't read his expression, but it woke the butterflies in her belly all over again.

All the survival manuals said sharing body warmth was a very effective way of raising body temperature. Gianluca would have felt happier if the instincts that were telling him to grab for that soft warmth came under the heading of survival.

He knew different. He had never stopped wanting Poppy Ramsay and Aurelia had known it... Oh, not the name but she had known that there was *someone—I can't compete with a memory, Luca.*

The citrusy perfume of Poppy's shampoo lingering in his nostrils, the words returned to haunt him as Gianluca turned abruptly towards the window where half the panes had shattered during the second blast of noise.

Poppy watched as he walked barefoot through the shards of broken glass on the floor. Not only did he possess catlike grace, but catlike instincts as he picked his way unerringly through the debris.

Gianluca assessed the damage. It appeared superficial inside at least. Luckily only one window was damaged; the wind whistled through the panes of broken glass; rain water was already pooling on the floor.

Poppy pressed a hand to her lips as he poked his head through the broken window, his skin coming perilously close to the wicked jagged fragments still adhering to the frame.

Bracing his hands on the stone window sill, he raised himself an inch or so higher and, narrowing his eyes against the driving rain, scanned the area for clues.

He did not have to look far for an explanation. On the ground not far from the window lay the remnants of a section of cast-iron guttering complete with rusted fixings. One large piece had travelled farther and as another flash lit up the landscape he had a glimpse of the considerable damage done to a Victorian glasshouse that, according to the tales he had been told, in its day had supplied the household with fruit and contained a renowned collection of rare orchids.

No wonder it had sounded like Armageddon.

Gianluca pulled his head back inside, grunting softly as he lowered himself back into the room, blinking away the water that streamed into his eyes.

'It's just some guttering and a few slates. The greenhouse took a hit and part of the wall around the garden—'

Poppy shook her head, interrupting the list of damage. 'No, that went the winter before last.' The sheep now grazed what had once been a kitchen garden; that was where the walker who had broken his ankle had been injured. 'It's a bad storm. This sort of damage could have happened anywhere—it doesn't mean that the place is unsafe.'

He raised an eloquent brow but stayed silent.

'All right,' she sighed. 'You're right and the men in suits are right—the place is falling down, but, Luca, Gran loves it.' She clenched her fists as she added fiercely, 'We can't let her lose it.'

There was a perceptible pause. *'We won't.'*

The colour rushed to her face, scoring the smooth curves of her classical cheekbones. 'I didn't mean *we*.' There was no *we* any more. 'I don't expect you to... I have it covered—' A wildly optimistic claim that sounded lame even to her own ears.

'I know what you meant, Poppy.'

Good, she thought, *that makes one of us.*

'And I share your concern for your grandmother and this place.' He cast an affectionate glance around the room with its dust, peeling paintwork and eclectic mix of shabby furnishings. 'I want to help, that's why I'm here, but I suggest for the present we address ourselves to the more immediate challenge of keeping the rain outside?'

'Sounds like a plan.'

Poppy was surprised to find she actually felt some relief to realise that she wouldn't have to tackle Gran's legal nightmare single-handed. It might not be comfortable being around Luca, but it would be selfish as well as stupid if she let their history stand in the way of keeping Gran in her ancestral pile.

The odds were that Luca would pass on the problem to someone with a legal degree and loads of experience anyhow, but if he decided to take a more hands-on approach, well... *You'll just have to suck it up, Poppy*, she told herself sternly.

How hard could it be?

'I'll need to cover the broken panes...' He glanced around the room, frowning, not immediately seeing anything appropriate for the job.

Poppy, infected by the urgency in his manner, dropped to her knees. It was good to be able to focus on something practical.

'How about this?' she asked, pulling out the old crate set in a corner beside the inglenook. She began to remove the kindling and old newspapers her gran kept in it before turning it around for Gianluca's approval.

He gave a grunt of grudging assent. 'That might do,' he admitted. 'Very resourceful, *cara*.'

She ignored the inappropriate endearment and slid the crate across the floor. 'I was a Girl Guide.'

'I was not a Boy Scout.'

No surprise there, she thought, watching as Luca stopped it with his foot and then, bracing one side against his knee, applied pressure. The loosely tacked seams stretched and gave with a splintering sound. Luca had never been the *joining* sort—it was people who were drawn to him.

He loosened a side and pulled it free before holding it out towards the window and sizing it up, one eye closed.

'Not bad,' he conceded.

While he wedged it in one of the gaps, peeling off a few strips of thin wood to force it into the available space, Poppy addressed the partially dismembered crate, freeing another panel.

His dark brows lifted when she handed it to him.

'It's called teamwork,' she told him, squatting back on her heels to watch him casually climb onto a table and coax it into the appropriate place with his fist.

'It should hold,' he decided, surveying his work.

Conscious of a tight feeling in her chest, Poppy watched him jump off the table and pad across the icy room towards her bare-footed and bare-chested, his body bearing visible evidence of his dramatic unorthodox journey. With a shadow on his jaw and his dark hair wet and slicked back, he brought an image of swashbuckling pirate to her mind.

His feet stopped inches away from her. She supposed the downside of having a husband who looked like Luca was knowing that, wedding band or not, women were going to be throwing themselves at his feet wherever he went. Well, she was one woman that Aurelia did not have to worry about Poppy thought as she got to her feet with more haste than grace.

She tilted her head back and found that Luca was staring at her.

'Stop looking at me like that!' She was too unnerved by the intensity of his scrutiny to censor her demand.

His massive shoulders lifted fractionally. 'You still look so young,' he marvelled. 'Seven years and you look...' He shook his head, adding, 'It is remarkable.'

'It's actually a nuisance,' she retorted. 'You have no idea how often I get asked for proof of age and people don't take you seriously professionally when you look like a teenager.'

His lips twisted into a smile. 'When you are as old as me you will take it as a compliment.'

'You're only five years older than me, Luca.'

He always had been hung up about her age.

When she had been going through the classic dumpee phase of 'What is wrong with me? What have I done?' Poppy had wondered if maybe the ingénue innocent stuff had been a factor, the novelty had worn off and he had just found it boring. These days her self-esteem, even after the recent humiliating Rupert incident, was a lot more robust.

'Chronologically maybe, but in experience, *cara*, I'm a hundred years older than you.' His sloe-dark eyes slid to her mouth as he wondered about her rites of passage into womanhood and the men who had been part of it. If things had been different it could have been him, him initiating Poppy in the art of lovemaking.

A wave of familiar self-disgust washed over him. If he had spent more time and energy trying to make his marriage work and less thinking about the lost opportunity, Aurelia might not have felt so isolated and alone.

She might be alive.

He had ruined two lives, but Poppy at least had escaped his toxic influence. She had moved on from the infatuation.

She had her own life yet…he couldn't stop thinking about how she had felt in his arms moments earlier… as if she belonged there, a perfect fit.

Too much truth, Luca, said the voice in his head as he closed his eyes, suddenly tired of his thoughts, tired of the situation—just tired.

'Luca.'

He opened his eyes. 'Come on, let's get this thing done.' The muscles along his strong jaw quivered and tightened as he snatched up a piece of light splintered wood and turned back to the window.

Feeling her eyes on his back as he applied himself to the task.

CHAPTER FOUR

IT TOOK him another five minutes to complete the running repairs. When there was not enough wood to cover the last broken pane he resorted to stretching the jacket he had been wearing earlier across the gap.

As she handed it up to him when requested the name on the hand-sewn designer label had made Poppy break her silence. 'Are you sure?'

Gianluca misinterpreted her comment. 'It's not perfect but it's better than nothing.'

'It'll be ruined.'

He gave a very Latin shrug and looked perplexed by the comment. 'So? It is a jacket. If it makes you feel any better it already is ruined—I have been swimming in it.'

'True.'

'Not bad,' he decided, angling a last critical look at his handiwork before he rejoined her. 'Actually the timing of this was pretty good.'

Poppy shook her head. She'd heard of positive spin, but to suggest having the place fall around their ears was good timing seemed quite a stretch. 'You think?'

'Nobody was outside. That gutter weighs a ton. It

could have come down at any time, not just in a storm. And if anyone had been under it at the time...'

The colour blenched from Poppy's face. 'Gran, you mean,' she whispered.

Silently cursing himself for not anticipating her re-action, he shook his head. 'No, of course not.'

Poppy shook her head. 'You're lying, Luca, that's exactly what you meant and you're right.' Her voice hardened with self-reproach as she added bitterly, 'God, what were we thinking letting her live here all alone?'

'It is Isabel's choice.'

'She would be more comfortable living somewhere smaller, more convenient, a cottage in the village with people around if she got sick...'

'It would be much more sensible,' he agreed. 'But she'd hate it and you know it.'

'I don't care. I just want her to be safe.' She dropped her head into her hands and gritted, 'I should have car-ried on searching!'

'Do not be absurd.'

'It's true! I shouldn't have come indoors the mo-ment it started drizzling. You said yourself the place is a death trap—she could be lying there now...'

'Poppy...'

Poppy's head came up with a jerk, her blazing eyes raking his face. 'And don't act like you care. If you were half a man you'd be out there now looking for her... Well, if you won't...' her chest heaving with emotion, she struggled for breath as she pulled the half-fastened zip of her padded jacket all the way up to her chin and took a deep defiant breath '...I will!' she announced fiercely.

'No, you won't!' he responded with equal decision. Holding her eyes, he caught hold of the zipper and tugged until the jacket opened to reveal a soft blue sweater and gentle curves.

Poppy swung away. 'You can't stop me!'

The hands that came to rest heavily on her shoulders ruined her big exit and illustrated quite clearly that he could stop her. Physically there was no contest.

With an impatient frown she swung round, tilting her head back to deliver a narrow-eyed glare.

'Stop it!' she warned. 'Or I'll...'

'Scream and yell some more, possibly stamp your little foot?' he drawled.

In an embarrassed flash she realised how appallingly she was behaving. 'I'm behaving like a child, aren't I? Sorry...' she added with disarming sincerity.

'You're upset.'

There was a lot to be upset about, and until Luca had walked in Poppy had thought she was handling it pretty well. There had been no other option. If she'd lost it there would have been nobody to pick up the pieces—then Luca had arrived and she'd morphed into some needy little girl expecting him to make things better.

'And you're right, there's no point assuming the worst—it's just been...' When she started speaking her voice was satisfactorily tough and capable; before it faded away to nothing it had become a whisper.

Her glance locked with Luca's Latin dark-framed eyes—eyelashes like that were so wasted on a man—and thought, *When did I last eat?*

Her clenched fists fell to her sides as she heard his deep voice above the heavy rapid thud of her heart; the rich accented tones seemed to be coming from a long way off.

Massive blood sugar dip! 'I feel a bit...'

Poppy found her chin on her chest.

'You *need* to take a deep breath.'

He nodded approval as he felt her shudder beneath his fingers; her shoulders remained rigid. She was wound up tight enough to shatter.

'I don't faint,' she protested weakly. 'I just...'

'Humour me, just do it.'

Poppy closed her eyes and exhaled, her fractured sigh terminating in a cough.

'Now another.'

Poppy nodded and responded automatically to the throaty instructions. She was relieved when he let her head up.

'Better now?'

She blinked and gave a shamefaced nod of assent, shaking her silky hair back from her face. 'Perhaps,' she suggested with a forced laugh to cover her embarrassment as she dug a half-bar of chocolate from her pocket, 'it's time to change the medication...'

Her joke was met with an unresponsive stare.

Gianluca watched as she peeled back the foil off the chocolate bar and pushed several squares into her mouth before turning her head to blot a tear running down her cheek against the wool of her soft baby-blue jumper.

It was as if the years had slipped away and he were standing there, music in the background, the flower from his lapel crushed between his fingers as he breathed through a rampant blast of the most primal sexual hunger he had ever experienced—and not for his bride.

Dio, he had no idea what ingredient Poppy had that

no other women he had met had that affected him this way.

'For the record, I do care what happens to Isabel.'

She gave a shamefaced grimace. 'I know that and she's very fond of you. And *for the record* I'm not normally this pathetic, I just have a blood-sugar thing. Nothing serious, but it's not so good if I skip meals.' She winced as the hands that lay heavily on her shoulders tightened, driving the chill of his fingers through her sweater. 'You're freezing!'

Luca dismissed her comment with a shrug. 'I'm fine.'

'You look terrible.' Her guilt-ridden glance took in the dark flush etched along the ridges of his razor-sharp cheekbones—he was clearly halfway to pneumonia. 'You need to get warm.' *My prioritising definitely needs work.* 'I'll see if I can find something upstairs for you. There might be something of Dad's.'

She was halfway across the room when he whistled.

Poppy swung back, her eyes wide, not mistaking the piercing sound as a sign of admiration. 'Flora!' She tilted her head in a listening attitude, half expecting to hear the sound of paws on the floor. 'If she'd been outside she'd have come or barked when I called.' Her gran's exuberant border collie was extremely obedient.

'So Flora isn't here. Correct me if I'm wrong, but does that not suggest that Isabel isn't here either?'

Poppy gave a sigh of relief. 'Flora never leaves her side.'

'For what it's worth my theory is that your grandmother, knowing that the storm was coming, decided sensibly to leave, taking her dog with her, to sit it out in the village. Think about it,' he suggested.

Poppy did, and what he said made sense. She couldn't understand why she hadn't thought of it herself.

'You *really* think so, Luca…?'

'You don't?'

'You might have forgotten but my gran is pretty stubborn.' Too stubborn to admit a mere storm could get the better of her…?

'True, but Aunt Isabel is also, as I recall, realistic and a Highlander. She has a healthy respect for the forces of nature.'

Poppy nodded in agreement. 'She spent most of the really bad snow in the village last year.'

'There you go, then.'

'Do you really think that she's safe, Luca…?'

'Don't you?'

'I want to.'

Gianluca lowered his gaze because looking at the lines of strain etched into the soft, smooth face was fuelling his growing desire to soothe them away.

'What's stopping you? You were, as I recall, always an optimist…a regular Pollyanna ready with a positive spin.' It was a quality he had teased her about but one that had secretly pleased him.

'Thanks, Luca,' she said gruffly.

One dark brow lifted to a questioning angle as he met the uncomplicated gratitude shining in her eyes. He swallowed and looked away quickly. 'For what?'

'If you hadn't been here…it would have been…a lot worse.' *God, now there is a sentence I never thought I'd hear myself say.* 'You should take off the rest of your clothes.'

The unexpected addition drew a startled growl of laughter from his throat.

The sexy sound made her blush. Ignoring the gleam in the stare levelled at her burning face and the image forming in her head of him naked, Poppy kept her chin high.

'I was just thinking out loud, not that I was thinking about you with...you're in wet clothes...' *Stop digging, Poppy.* 'You should take them off,' she elaborated with shaky dignity. 'As a precaution.'

As a precaution Gianluca intended to keep his pants on for the present, though if he moved he doubted they would conceal the level of his arousal. He had not been in this situation since he was a teenager in the grip of rampant hormones.

'It's probably warmer in the kitchen,' she mumbled, nodding in the direction of the connecting door. She had been contemplating retreating there when he had arrived. 'I'll go and...ah, find...' *Just go, Poppy, before you make even more of a fool of yourself.*

Making her way down the spiral stone staircase a short while later, Poppy was unable to resist the impulse that made her pause and glance at her reflection in the old mirror at the bottom.

'Oh, God!'

And candlelight was notoriously kind!

The wild hair and pale face, the only evidence of the make-up she had applied many hours earlier the faint dark smudge rimming her eyes, it was just as well she was not out to impress—she had seen more attractive-looking scarecrows.

The big room was empty. Presumably Gianluca had followed her advice. The room actually was more welcoming than it had been thanks to the fire that had finally stopped smoking and begun burning cheerily.

Approaching the door into the kitchen, she paused, put down the stack of clothing she was carrying and began to push back the wispy strands of hair from her face. Midway through manically smoothing down her hair, Poppy stopped, her hand falling back to her sides and a horror-struck expression crossing her face.

Her frantic efforts to make herself look more presentable—especially considering the *married* person whose benefit they were for—struck Poppy as pitiable. She gave a snort of disgust and, clenching her jaw, muttered, 'Good idea, Poppy, because your biggest problem is *definitely* the state of your hair.'

Bending forward, she shook her head, digging her fingers into the mesh of almost-dry waves to complete the mussing-up process—childish maybe, and not on the face of it *totally* in keeping with the 'modern liberated woman' persona she had decided to adopt, but it made her feel better.

When she was satisfied she had undone any minor improvements there might have been she straightened up and scowling at the vanity that made her want to look good for a sexy man, picked up the folded clothes and opened the kitchen door with her elbow, walking down the stone step backwards.

Gianluca, who turned when the door creaked closed behind her, was standing in front of the ancient range in the kitchen, which up until recently her grandmother had cooked all her food on. These days she had a small electric cooker and even a microwave, but the monster still heated all the water and came in handy when the power failed.

In her absence he had followed her suggestion and divested himself of more wet garments. They now lay

in a sodden heap on the floor. She recognised his in-
novative outfit as the blanket flung across the saggy
sofa under the window and refused to speculate what,
if anything, remained under it.

He had wrapped the rough fabric around his waist
then thrown the spare fabric over one shoulder. As far
as she could tell the weight of the fabric was the only
thing holding it in place. He got full marks for the in-
genious use of limited resources.

On a personal level Poppy would have felt happier if
it had looked more...secure, though she had to admit it
was not a look many men could have pulled off, but then
even his worst enemy would have agreed that Gianluca
was not *any man*.

With the rough blanket thrown over his shoulder, his
strong shadowed jaw and wet, tousled dark hair he made
her think of the brooding heroes, men of few words but
hidden depths, in one of the old spaghetti westerns her
dad was addicted to. Poppy, who had watched them
with him when she was a child, retained a definite secret soft spot for cowboy boots or at least the idea of
the men who wore them.

'Any luck?' Gianluca stopped what he was doing and
turned around, his attention drawn to her hair, paler
now it was dry. Masses of soft honey-brown waves
rested on her shoulders and spilled down her narrow
back.

At his side his fingers flexed as he found himself
thinking of sinking his hands into the shining strands
and letting them fall through his fingers. He pushed
away the image of that cloud of hair against paler bare
skin and cleared his throat.

Poppy dumped the clothes she had managed to find

upstairs on the scrubbed table that took centre stage in the middle of the room.

'You might not think so.' Her father's old kilt was a few billion miles from the designer stuff she assumed he normally wore. 'But I found these.' She half turned her head, her glance brushing his face—at least that had been her intention, but her eyes showed a marked disinclination to move on.

Whoever said knowledge was power, it turned out they were wrong. Poppy knew she was staring and she couldn't do a damned thing about it!

Poppy had heard people talk about the 'X factor' when talking about the opposite sex; she had never really got it. Now she realised it was something you had to experience before you understood.

And she was experiencing it, and the accompanying tight knot that went with it in the pit of her stomach. It wasn't just that he was an incredibly good-looking man; actually, she admitted, he was beautiful—how many men could look elegant wrapped in a blanket, for goodness' sake? But it was the concentrated raw masculinity he radiated that she had a problem with.

Her chest lifted in a silent sigh as her gaze strayed towards his mouth, his beautiful, sensually moulded lips. Poppy doubted if there were a woman alive who could look at that mouth without wondering a little what it would be like to be kissed by those lips.

She knew exactly what it felt like.

The thought was floating through her mind when the sudden shrill whistle of the bubbling kettle on the hob jolted her back to reality.

She blinked and walked quickly across to the range.

On the point of reaching for the whistling kettle her hand was abruptly dragged away.

Gianluca bit out a curse in Italian and raked her face with dark eyes that contained fury.

Poppy, bewildered by his inexplicable action and the anger that appeared to have materialised out of thin air, responded to the glare and the restraining hand on her wrist with an equally fiery glower of her own.

'Just what *exactly* do you think you are doing?' he ground out furiously.

In the background the kettle continued to shrill spitting out steam as the pressure built. Poppy too was feeling the effects of building pressure. There was no outlet for the mad swirl of confusing emotions that swelled up inside her in a thick choking tide.

It was as if the trauma of the day had woken up her dormant hormones, and woken them up big time—the event being timed to cause the maximum embarrassment. Still the situation was doable so long as the attraction remained physical, which obviously it would because she was not the same person she had been at eighteen and Luca…she'd had a few glimpses of the young man she had fallen for, but this older Luca was much…*harder* in every way.

She held herself rigid and thought, *You need to get a grip, girl,* as she transferred her gaze from his face to the fingers circling her wrist and back to his face.

Her eyes slid to his mouth. She wanted to kiss him so badly it hurt.

She needed more sugar.

That's not what you need.

'You're hurting me.'

Gianluca looked down into her face, the expression

in his own heavy-lidded eyes giving no clues as to what he was thinking. Without a word he released her, then, holding her eyes, he tipped his head in a jerky motion that might have indicated apology.

Still holding her gaze, he picked up a folded tea towel and ostentatiously wrapped it around the exposed hot metal of the kettle handle before he lifted it off the hot-plate.

'I am assuming that would have hurt more.'

Her eyes shot wide in realisation.

He stopped abruptly, his eyes skimming her pale face before he turned away, clenching out a stressed, *'Madre di Dio!'* Before adding an equally abrupt, 'I couldn't find any coffee.'

'Gran doesn't drink it. She only buys it in for visitors. Thanks for...' Feeling like a total idiot, she nodded awkwardly towards the kettle and flexed the fingers of her right hand that would have been burnt but for his intervention.

His tipped his head. 'You are welcome.'

The water might have stopped boiling but the same could not be said of the atmosphere that seethed with tension. Poppy tugged at the neck of her sweater and, almost suffocated by the silence, blurted, 'I got the damned clothes—will you put them on...*please*...?'

His dark eyes swivelled her way as he retorted without missing a beat, 'Why—so that you can take them off?'

Poppy gave a gasp of outrage, guiltily conscious as she did so of the heat low in her pelvis. 'Are you flirting with me?'

'Was I not meant to?'

Unable to meet his knowing gaze, her eyes fell. Did

he have a point? Hadn't she been sending out mixed messages?

She was uncomfortably conscious that her entire attitude had been and continued to be pretty schizophrenic about Luca. Ever since he'd appeared emotions had been see-sawing dramatically as she struggled against a determination to keep him at arm's length physically and emotionally and an equally strong inclination to pull him close in every way.

'You're married and I don't—'

'Don't what, Poppy?' he asked, the normal warm timbre of his voice harsh as he pinned her with a piercing contemptuous stare. '*Dio*, but you used to be a hell of a lot more honest about what you wanted.' The longer she looked at him as if he were some big bad wolf, the more Gianluca felt the urge to act like one, take her face between his hands and plunder those plump pink lips. Not totally rational, but the heavy dull ache of arousal in his groin was hard to think beyond.

'I don't want you!'

Before she knew it he was beside her. Without saying a word he planted one hand in the small of her back, the other on the curve of her hip, and with negligent ease dragged her to him.

She was too startled by his actions to resist—that was her story and she was sticking to it!

He arched an expressive brow and lowered his mouth to hers, his dark eyes glittering with insolent challenge. 'No…?'

A whimper caught in Poppy's throat as he parted her lips and slid his tongue inside her mouth with erotic precision.

'Luca…' The pent-up longing in her cry was lost in

his mouth as he deepened the penetration possessively, tasting her like a starving man with a hot passion that she found both intoxicating and terrifying.

As fire licked along her nerve endings she kissed him back, pressing closer to the lean, hard length of him, not even trying to pretend she didn't want this… didn't want it a lot.

She was shaking and burning up from the inside out when he finally pulled back, growling low in his throat, then moving back to the tea preparation acting as if nothing had happened. Only the exaggerated rise and fall of his chest and the slight tremor in his hands any indication anything out of the ordinary had just occurred—maybe it was ordinary for Luca these days.

'If I made you think I wanted you to do that…I'm sorry. But for the record I don't—'

'No, let me guess.' He turned his head, his dark insolent glance skimming across her face as he made the pretence of thinking hard. 'You don't kiss married men.'

Poppy made her face like stone, not wanting him to see how much he was hurting her. 'No, I don't,' she concurred, not about to apologise.

If he reacted with this sort of derision to something she didn't think many people would view as either a problem or a shortcoming Poppy could only imagine how he'd react if he knew about her intimacy issues!

She smiled wryly to herself. Even in the privacy of her own thoughts she couldn't come right out and say it—*I'm Poppy and I'm a twenty-five-year-old virgin.* In the words of the only friend she had ever confided in on the subject, she was a girl who bolted at the final fence.

Luca gave an unpleasant laugh.

'God, Luca, you really have changed,' she exclaimed, wondering sadly if she had ever really known him at all.

She had never put Luca on a pedestal when they were together, so it made no sense at all for her to feel so utterly disillusioned now, when she wasn't even the injured party, Aurelia was. Poppy felt desperately ashamed that she'd sent out the sort of messages that had made him think she'd be up for some light-hearted flirtation and maybe more... The kiss, she recalled with a shudder, had not felt light-hearted and neither had her response—her body was still quivering with lustful aftershocks.

'There's no need to sleep with married men because generally I find there's no shortage of unmarried ones.' She didn't add they all had limited patience with someone who was not willing to *put out*—not all phrased it that way but even the nicest got less understanding when several dates gave back little beyond a goodnight kiss.

'I'm not married.'

This stopped her cold.

'You're divorced?' Now *that* had never occurred to her. Poppy was not sure what she felt about this revelation...not immediate joy.

'No, not divorced.'

'Then?'

'Aurelia is dead.'

The shock of his bald statement drew a raw gasp from Poppy. 'I'm so s-sorry,' she stuttered, wincing inwardly at the sheer inadequacy of her words. Her legs, the consistency of cotton wool, gave and her bottom hit the seat of the wooden chair hard enough to send it skating backwards across the flagged floor. Grabbing the seat with both hands, she shuffled it back to the table.

'How…? Was it sudden?'

He poured tea into a mug and dug a spoon into a bowl of sugar. 'I killed her… Sugar? No, you don't, do you?'

Poppy stared at him, incredulity nailing her to her seat… Had she heard right? Had he really said what she thought he had…?

'Yes…no…you can't just say *that* and…drink *tea*!'

'There is no coffee.'

The word play did not impress Poppy, who watched him unloop the swathe of fabric from his shoulders and pull the heavy sweater from the top of the pile on the table.

'Come on, Luca, you can't drop something like that on me and leave it at that.' It did not even cross her mind to believe that he might be guilty of the crime he suggested.

'What is there to say?'

Struggling not to yell in response to his nihilistic shrug, she said firmly, 'You didn't kill anyone.'

'How do you know this?'

'If you had you wouldn't be walking around, you'd be in jail.'

'Your faith in the justice system is charming, but somewhat misguided.'

'Not the justice system—you…I know you, Luca…'

She saw something flash in his expressive eyes before his lashes came down in a luxuriant screen. 'I am responsible for Aurelia's death, end of story, but if it helps you the coroner called it suicide.' But he knew different.

They could talk of the balance of her mind and discuss her long history of mental health problems, so severe that she had once been sectioned, but Luca knew that if he had not married her Aurelia would still be alive today...not happy, maybe, but alive.

'Aurelia killed herself!' The shock of discovery left a conflicted Poppy feeling disorientated. Tears sprang to her eyes as an image of the beautiful brunette on her wedding day drifted across her vision. 'Oh, Luca, that must have been awful for you.'

Luca dragged out a chair and sat down heavily, resting his chin on steepled fingers. The sympathy glowing in Poppy's luminous eyes made him respond harshly. 'It was a great deal more awful for Aurelia.'

In such cases it had often seemed to Poppy that it was the people left behind who suffered most, but she kept this reflection to herself. 'When did this happen?' she asked quietly.

'Eighteen months ago.'

His father had come up to him after the funeral and, unusually for a physically undemonstrative man, had hugged him.

'Sad, so sad...she was a troubled spirit. You have to believe me, Luca, that I had no idea about the breakdown she had while she was at finishing school, or I would never have encouraged the marriage. The family kept it quiet. Alessandro told everyone she was attending a cordon bleu course in Paris...said she'd graduated top of her class... If I had had any idea...but no matter—at least you're still young. There's plenty of time left for you to find someone else, to have a family.'

It had been the sentiment underlying much of the

words of sympathy that day–he was young; he would move on.

Luca fully intended to move on but not in the same direction.

He had left his father in no doubt that there would be no wife, no children. There would be nobody in his life he could hurt or let down—of this Luca was positive.

Poppy felt a wave of helplessness as she watched him. It was clear that Luca was not in this room, he was far away, and whatever thoughts going through his head clearly dark.

She sat and waited. The tea in her mug was lukewarm when he finally broke the lengthening silence. 'I should have known.'

'How could you have known?' Poppy protested.

'It wasn't the first time.'

Poppy pressed a hand to her mouth. 'Oh, Luca!'

'That,' he explained, 'happened after she miscarried the first time, a plea for help...attention, they said, she wasn't serious. I was away...I was always away.'

Poppy, reluctant to interrupt him, bit back the protest that rose to her lips in response to the self-loathing in his voice.

'On the day it happened I was meant to arrive home that afternoon.' His face was dark as he relived the events. 'If I had they could have washed out her stomach again and everything would have been all right, but I didn't get home. I didn't want to,' he admitted heavily. 'I wanted to avoid another inevitable discussion about babies.

'She desperately wanted a baby but she couldn't carry them to term and the doctors said the repeat pregnancies were affecting her health—not, as it turned out, as badly as a bottle of antidepressants and wine but…' His head fell back, exposing the long strong column of his brown neck as he dragged a hand through his dark hair.

'You know the crazy thing…?'

Poppy, longing to banish that bleakness from his eyes, shook her head, feeling powerless. What could she say that would not sound clichéd?

'She never even liked babies…children.'

Not sure if she was meant to rebut this claim, Poppy remained silent.

'But she knew I did and she felt it was her *duty.*' He turned his head, screening his expression from her, but Poppy could hear the pain in his voice as he added, 'Aurelia always tried to please…please everyone.'

She was horrified by the picture he painted. It was clear that Aurelia, the poor woman, had had some serious mental health issues and she and Luca had not enjoyed the sort of fairy-tale marriage that Poppy had always imagined. She had envied them their perfect lives.

'It was a tragic accident, Luca, but not your fault— you must see that.'

Everyone had said that and everyone was wrong. 'Whose fault is it, then?'

'Does it have to be anyone's fault?'

'Yes! I was a terrible husband!' His fierce expression dared Poppy to disagree. 'Some men should stay single and I am one of them.'

As she watched he blinked and blinked again, his dark eyes focusing on her face as if he were realising for the first time who he was talking to. He looked startled to see anyone there, let alone her.

She could almost see him pulling back, withdrawing. 'You don't want to know any of this.' He frowned, passed a hand across his eyes and added almost angrily, 'I've no idea why I told you.'

'Sometimes it's therapeutic to talk,' she offered gently.

Had he talked to anyone or had he just been walking around with all that guilt? It made her heart break just thinking about it.

'And sometimes it is self-indulgent,' he countered grimly.

Poppy took up the mug on the table and nursed it between her hands, looking at him over the rim. 'So you think if you ignore stuff it will just—' she pursed her lips and mouthed softly '—poof, vanish. It doesn't work that way.'

'We all have our own way of dealing. Not everyone wants to *share* their feelings—' his lips thinned in scornful distaste '—or pay a shrink to hear them vent.'

'So what has been your way of dealing, Luca? Besides just sucking it up?' The trouble with men like Luca, Poppy brooded darkly, was they equated silence with strength.

'Sex. I have discovered the joy of one-night stands.' What could be better than satisfying a basic human need with someone who wanted nothing from you? The gratification was brief and left a gnawing sense of dissatisfaction but Luca was philosophical—a man could not have everything.

From where Poppy was sitting she could see precious little evidence of joy!

Dark head tilted to one side, he studied her face. 'You look shocked.' It was preferable to her looking at him as if he were a charity case.

'I am.'

His lips thinned. 'I never had you down as a prude.'

'I just never thought it was your...style, Luca, to act as though sex is some sort of game or treat women as toys.'

Of course, she knew he had a high sex drive—Luca had admitted freely to her when they began dating that he had been sexually active at an early age, but when he'd said he had never been promiscuous she had believed him.

Being a highly sexed man didn't make him callous or inconsiderate.

CHAPTER FIVE

'I AM sorry I have not lived up to your high expectations, *cara*.'

'Maybe it's your own expectations you haven't lived up to, Luca…?'

It had been a stab in the dark but his expression suggested Poppy had come closer to the truth than Luca liked. She was not surprised; she couldn't imagine the Luca she had once known turning into a man who was satisfied with a series of shallow relationships.

'I think we have exhausted the topic of my personal life.'

Poppy had the impression they had only just scratched the surface, but then with Luca there had always been more below the surface than was visible… Her eyes drifted over his face and she sighed. He was a very complex man.

Luca gave a twisted smile. 'And anyway we should perhaps leave some sordid details for tomorrow in case we run out of conversation.'

Shock flashed across Poppy's face as she shot upright in her chair. 'Tomorrow! You think we'll still be here then?'

Luca took a certain savage satisfaction in her horrified reaction. 'What weather forecast did you tune into?' He got to his feet and went back to the stove, dropping a tea bag into his mug before adding water from the kettle. 'They were forecasting this weather would last several days.' Through half-closed eyelids he watched the last vestige of colour fade from her face.

'But we won't be stuck here that long!' As she spoke, keeping her voice carefully level, Poppy could feel the panic snapping at her heels.

'It is a distinct, a very distinct possibility.' His eyes dropped to her heaving bosom and he felt the hunger in his belly tighten. 'I can see the prospect fills you with joy.'

'It fills me with horror and unless you're totally insane it would you too!' She gave a fractured little sigh and forced a determined smile. 'Weather reports are notoriously inaccurate—we might wake up tomorrow morning and find ourselves in the middle of a heatwave.'

Which left the night...which Poppy was more nervous about than she cared to admit.

'It might...' A fresh squall of hailstones hit the west-facing window and he added, 'Or maybe not.'

She squeezed her eyes closed and pleaded, 'Can we talk about something other than the weather?'

The request drew a sardonic smile from Luca. 'That is extremely un-British of you,' he reproached with mock shock. 'But fine, so what about you, Poppy? Are you in a committed relationship?' he asked, his tone mocking the final words.

Not the change of subject she had had in mind!

'Me...?' She gave an uncomfortable shrug. 'Not exactly...'

It gave Luca a certain sense of redress to see that Poppy was less comfortable with discussing her personal life than she had been his. He resented the way she had tricked him into opening up and saying things that he had not said to anyone.

'I was with someone…sort of.'

In light of what he had just revealed the recent traumatic events in her personal life seemed pretty mild.

It had not seemed that way at the time—to find out, along with the rest of the building, that your possible virginity was the subject of a wager was bad. But when you also learnt that the really nice man you had been dating had nominated himself as the person to find out was beyond humiliating!

Rupert had seemed so nice and, not guessing his sordid ulterior motive, she had been flattered and even wondered if this time she might…? Clearly he had thought so too, according to the email that had been intended for the group of creepy friends who risked money on his findings.

Tonight was the night, Rupert had announced triumphantly, and it, or rather *she*, was a sure thing, Poppy had read along with the entire building. Rupert's crude boast via email had inadvertently reached a lot more than his target audience.

Rupert had lost his bet and she had become an object of pity. On the surface people were sympathetic and even indignant on her behalf but underneath she knew they were all wondering if it was true and if it was— *why*?

On more than one occasion Poppy had found herself fighting the need to justify herself and it infuriated her. The situation with her sex life or rather lack of it had never previously unduly concerned her. She had always assumed that it would happen at the right time with the right person, but what if the right time and person had been and gone and her chance was missed…?

She realised that her teenage experience with Luca had made her cautious about following her instincts, which was maybe why she always bolted when things began to get serious. Yet at the same time part of her had longed to experience that magical moment when she Luca had stepped off the ferry looking tanned and fit and his smile had felt like a stomach punch—she was in love.

She had never felt the stomach punch again and her caution had meant she had never gone looking for it—that, she decided, had been her mistake.

She had to be more proactive and less picky—nothing desperate like throwing herself at the first man who came her way, obviously, but she was going to put herself out there.

God, but she *hated* that phrase!

One thing was certain: she was never going to be in a position like the recent one that had resulted in her handing in her notice rather than continue to be the subject of sniggers and speculation.

She was going to rid herself of her wretched virginity; it had become a burden.

All she needed now was a man.

Luca patted the stack of garments on the table. 'So what happened?'

Poppy tilted her head to return the stare of her interrogator. 'It just didn't work out.' Luca was a man.

'So have you ever been engaged…?'

Shocked and excited by the idea taking hold in her feverish brain, Poppy shook her head.

'If you want something doing,' her dad always said, 'go to the best!' If you applied the same principle to sex... Her heavy-lidded stare slid to the sensual curve of his strong mouth... Poppy's own lips tingled. Luca had to be in the running for that title.

'No, never.'

He was free and by his own admission he was into casual sex these days...though probably not virgins...

'Aunt Isabel said you work for Bateman and Latimer... that's impressive.'

'Gran said?' Poppy's brow pleated into a perplexed frown. Her gran never told her anything about Luca; presumably she knew about what had happened to Aurelia and she hadn't said a word. 'Well, yes, I did, but I handed in my notice recently. Phil is setting up on his own and he's asked me to join him.'

'Phil...?'

'Someone I met on my gap year.'

A look of shock passed across his lean face. 'You had a gap year.' He stopped and lowered his eyes.

Of course she had a gap year—her life had gone on after him... Poppy had met people, seen things...slept with boys.

'And you kept in touch. That's...nice,' he observed through a clenched smile. Poppy did not appear to notice the insincerity in his comment.

'Actually we ended up at the same university.'

In Luca's head the words translated as 'we slept together at university'.

'He's an accountant too.'

'Interesting.' Everyone knew that accountants were boring—the male ones, at least.

'The firm he was working for kept his job open while he took time off last year to join an expedition to the arctic. He could have had a partnership if he stayed on but he finds the atmosphere restrictive.'

'A strange thing to do in this job market—he sounds reckless.' Luca found himself disliking this unknown accountant with a sideline in exploring more by the second.

Poppy gave a vague nod, not totally committed to this conversation; her thoughts were elsewhere. 'That's the reason, according to Phil, that we'd make a good partnership. My more sensible approach will balance his recklessness.'

'And will you?'

Exactly what she was asking herself.

Would she sleep with Luca?

Luca found the veiled look she gave him annoying.

Ruthlessly suppressing her instinct to blurt out her great idea, Poppy carried her mug to the sink and began to scrub it hard enough to wash the painted roses on the china.

Previous experience with Luca had taught her the necessity of schooling her desire to rush in without thinking, all enthusiasm and no planning. And then there was the question of her motivation...did motivation matter?

She was after all totally over Luca—on an emotional level at least. Physically she still wanted to rip off his clothes, but that hardly made her unique—Luca was an incredibly sexy man—and it was positive plus when you were talking about going to bed with someone.

Not anyone—Luca. You couldn't ignore the history and could she run the risk of dredging up old feelings? The feelings were stone dead.

He might not want to have sex with her...? She thought of the kiss and her mouth went dry... *He did.*

She closed her eyes, not noticing that the water she was holding the mug under was ice cold. Her fingers were numb when she eventually switched off the flow.

Pity there was not a similar switch in her head, she mused, to turn off her thoughts that continued to go round and round in never-decreasing circles.

'No hot water?'

She turned around and found Luca was standing right behind her. Expecting him to move back, she paused; he didn't.

'Your fingers are blue, Poppy.'

'They're fine.' Evading his touch, Poppy tucked her hands across her chest. She could have backed up and made a detour but that would have been admitting something; instead she lifted her chin and sucked in a breath in an effort to avoid contact. She squeezed between him and the table.

'Hot water! Actually there's plenty of hot water—the wonders of an old-fashioned immersion tank.' She gave a bright smile. 'And a hot bath is just what you need to warm you up.'

It would also give her a cooling-off period, to weigh her options or at least breathe freely without his disturbing presence. 'I'll let you have first dibs at the bathroom.'

Luca's brows lifted in response to her enthusiasm. 'Very generous,' he said drily. 'A man might almost be forgiven for thinking you want to get rid of him...?'

Poppy didn't respond to the silky innuendo in his drawl. Instead she went into practical mode.

'You know where the bathroom is. I left some candles burning while I was up there—oh, and I ran a bath. It'll be cold now...' The fire had been meant to take a few minutes to light and then Gianluca had arrived and she had totally forgotten about her plans to take a hot bath.

'There are some matches on the table at the bottom of the stairs if you need them, and candles.' Poppy had discovered a store of candles that would see them through to the next decade! 'Just leave me some hot water.'

A wicked gleam appeared in his eyes. 'We could always share?' He had intended to make her laugh, but when her eyes darkened with the desire she could not hide his half-smile faded.

A pulse of lust slammed through his body.

Poppy forced a stiff smile. 'Were you always this predictable?'

Almost as predictable as the reaction of her body that seemed to have been programmed to react to him on a sexual level... She'd always thought that happened because she loved him; now she realised that it was actually a chemical thing.

'The offer stands,' he drawled, directing one last knee-trembling, smouldering stare at her face before exiting the room.

'The bathroom is free!'

It was half an hour later when the call echoed down the stairs. Poppy had now decided the idea of sleeping with Luca was a crazy one—maybe the craziest she had ever had.

It was a relief to have made a decision.

As tempting as the thought of sinking into a hot bath and washing off the accumulated grime was at that moment, the possibility of bumping into Luca in any state of undress caused Poppy to delay responding immediately to the invitation.

After a few minutes she took a candle, and went up the stone steps. The candles she had lit in the stone-wall embrasures still flickered as she made her way to the bathroom, a barn of a room containing an enormous old claw-footed cast-iron bathtub that took centre stage.

Tapping first on the half-open door to ensure it was empty, she went in. The room was empty but filled with steam from its recent occupation.

'I could do with a hand here!'

The request for assistance came from one of the numerous bedrooms off the hallway.

'I presume *you* know how a kilt works.'

'It's not rocket science!' she yelled back, her voice echoing off the stone walls as she directed her reply in the general direction of his voice before stepping quickly into the bathroom.

Once inside she leaned against the door and, spotting a spare chair, wedged it under the handle before carefully putting her candle on the window sill beside the others burning there.

The first thing her glance lighted on as she checked out the room was the wet towels in the hamper and the dry ones folded neatly on the wooden towel rail. She was forming a grudging approval of the fact that, despite the hundreds of flunkies he had to have, Luca did not expect others to pick up after him when her glance lighted on the clothes she had taken from her holdall earlier and laid out ready to change into.

They were there exactly where she had left them, still neatly laid out on a stool: clean jeans, dry socks, a sweater and there, right on top, the pair of shocking-pink pants and tartan silk bra—just because nobody saw her underclothes had never seemed a reason to Poppy not to have some fun with them.

She closed her eyes and groaned. She had totally forgotten she had put them there when she had offered him the first bath! The thought of Luca seeing those items, touching them even, sent a rush of heat through her body—they weren't even matching!

He might not even have noticed.

Sure he didn't!

Trying not to think about Luca or knickers and definitely not the two together, she turned on the hot water tap and, after tipping in a healthy slug of the herby scented bath oil her grandmother mixed herself, began to strip off.

Sinking into the warm fragrant water, she gave a sigh of pleasure as the tension drifted out of her body. She could have stayed there all night and might have had it not been for the draught blowing in through the rattling window.

As she topped up the cooling water again she realised why Luca had not lingered. Poppy had more staying power, though that staying power had more to do with a strong reluctance to rejoin Luca than a desire to linger in the lukewarm water.

She was trying to summon sufficient enthusiasm to leave the water, watching under heavy eyelids as the candles began to gutter one by one. There was just one left—the one she had carried into the room with her—

when she noticed the writing scrawled in the steam on the mirror.

I feel very differently about tartan now!
It was underlined.

To add insult to injury he had initialled it!

Rising in an angry rush from the water, she stepped out of the bath, her cheeks flushed as pink as her wet skin, and stalked across the room, her wet feet leaving puddles on the oak boards. Standing by the mirror, she wiped a hand angrily back and forth across the words written in the steam.

She finished dressing very quickly in the chilly room, pulling on the clean pair of jeans and a pale pink sweater that you could probably see her darker bra through, but as she wouldn't be showing him anything he hadn't already seen it was a wardrobe malfunction that didn't seem worth worrying about.

Poppy opened the door and let out a startled yelp. A tall, imposing, kilt-wearing Luca was blocking her path. 'What are you doing lurking like some...some...?' Incredibly sexy man, she silently completed—wow, her dad had never ever looked like that in a kilt! 'S-some *lurker*!'

She watched his sexy lips tremble and so did the sensitive nerves lining her pelvis.

'Is that actually a word?'

She found she didn't mind that he was laughing at her but she minded quite a lot that she sounded like a heavy breather. Her heart was vibrating so hard against her ribs she almost expected to hear a loud cracking sound as it broke its way out.

'It should be.' There should be a whole dictionary of new words specifically to describe him, she decided as she made a further covert study of what he was wearing.

He wore the sweater she had also supplied with the sleeves rolled up to reveal his sinewy, strong forearms lightly dusted with dark hair. The fine navy wool was pulled tighter across his well-developed chest than it had ever been intended to and was short enough to reveal a tantalising sliver of flat brown belly between the hem and the waistband of the kilt.

As he levered himself casually off the wall he'd been leaning up against and took a step towards her the kilt swung out at the knees, revealing a few extra inches of deeply muscled brown thigh.

'I was waiting for you.' He intercepted her stare, and added, 'You like the look?'

Her cheeks turned a guilty pink as she tightened her jaw and refused to rethink her earlier decision, well aware that any decision made when she was standing in the direct line of fire of his massive sexual magnetism could not be trusted.

There was very little point in liberating herself from her virgin status if she spent the next seven years recovering from the experience. She needed to move on, not jump backwards.

'You look more *Braveheart* than *Brigadoon*, and you found some socks...that's good...excellent...' *Babbling, Poppy, you're babbling.*

'Accessories are so important I always think,' he replied, straight-faced. 'Did you enjoy your bath? I was about to send in a search party.'

His eyes moved in a slow appreciative sweep down over her slim figure. The snug-fitting faded jeans she wore were topped with a pale candyfloss-pink sweater that drew attention to the swell of her breasts—actually his attention would have been drawn there no matter what she was wearing.

Smiling to himself as he recognised the faint outline of tartan visible through the pink, he let his eyes slide lower to the row of rib that cinched the sweater at waist level. The curves above were balanced by the feminine curves below. By the time his scrutiny had reached her tight, firm behind his breathing was all over the place.

His life did not bring him into contact with women who possessed Poppy's brand of sexy wholesomeness. It was easy to see men being bewitched by the combination of freshness and feistiness.

'I don't need an escort. I do know my way around.' Though probably not as well as Luca knew his way around the female body, she thought, and felt her nipples pinch into tight, painful awareness.

'I've lit the fire in my room. I thought I'd light one in yours and I wasn't sure—where are you going to sleep? And that wasn't an invitation...' His glance lingered thoughtfully on her flushed face as he added, 'Unless you want it to be?'

The sensual suggestion delivered in his inimitable deep throaty voice made her shiver.

Think very carefully about what you're passing on, said the voice in her head.

'I...I'm in the tower room, thanks, Luca, but the chimney there smokes like crazy.' She bit her lip and thought—*Forward, Poppy*. 'I'll put on an extra blanket.' As she began to turn jerkily away her elbow caught a vase holding a bunch of dusty dried flowers.

With a cry Poppy moved to catch it before it toppled,

Luca had moved with a similar intention. Her fingers were just closing over the vase when her body collided into a hard male body and with a gasp she opened her fingers.

Poppy heard it smash to the floor but did not look. Her eyes were held captive by the dark gaze burning into her. Combined with the feel of all that solid muscle and heat burning through her clothes it made her dizzy.

'I should get a dustpan.' Her voice sounded breathless and unfamiliar even to her own ears.

'Why?'

'Because there's glass on the floor.'

He lifted a strand of hair from her eyes. 'You're a beautiful woman.' His heavy lids dropped over his glittering stare as he inhaled deeply. '*Dio*, you smell good.'

'So do you,' Poppy breathed as he framed her face with his long fingers.

'You know we could be stuck here for days...' he stroked a long brown finger down her cheek '...and nights.'

Poppy turned her head and caught the tip of one of his fingers between her teeth and bit softly, then sucked, tasting salt.

She heard him gasp and thought, *Not bad for a learner.*

'Your skin is so soft,' he rasped running the finger she had just sucked damply up the curve of her pale throat towards her mouth and smiling when she shuddered in helpless reaction to his touch.

'Luca...' He stepped in closer and she could feel he was fully aroused and rock hard and she could feel it because he wanted her to.

'I've always wanted you.'

The throaty admission drew a choked little gasp from Poppy's aching throat. The sound increased the level of Luca's arousal another notch.

He touched the corner of her mouth with his thumb, then replaced the light pressure with his mouth, running his tongue across the surface of the moist interior of her pouting upper lip. 'I want to taste you...' he slurred against her mouth.

'Yes, please...that is, oh...' Desire exploded inside her, silencing the arguments in her head. Freed from the internal conflict and no longer restrained by common sense or logic, she gave herself up willingly to the hot flow of desire coursing through her veins, not thinking just feeling...reacting... Everything felt so right. She was amazed how right, but then it always had felt right with Luca.

'Good?' he suggested throatily.

She opened her heavy lids and looked at him with a kind of wonder in her eyes. 'I'm not going to bolt.'

'Good to know.'

She pressed closer and moaned as he kissed her properly, a hard kiss that stopped her heart for a split second before a surge of adrenaline got dumped in her bloodstream and her pulses started pounding all over her body, everywhere, in places she didn't know she had pulses.

He lifted his head and, breathing hard, looked into her flushed face. 'If we don't make the bedroom in the next sixty seconds I might not make it at all. I wouldn't want you to get carpet burn on my account.'

Just looking at him made her weak with longing. 'There's no carpet.'

His hands slid to her bottom and he pulled her in, breathing deep as he felt all that softness pressing against him. 'And wanting you is driving me slightly insane.'

CHAPTER SIX

LUCA swung her into his arms as if she weighed nothing. Poppy, her arms looped around his neck, was nuzzling the warm brown salty skin of his throat when he kicked open the door of a bedroom.

The room Luca had chosen was not as big as many in the castle, which made it only half the size of a football pitch, but the candles lined up along the window ledge and the logs crackling in the grate of the carved stone fireplace gave it an almost cosy feel.

Poppy barely registered these touches as Luca strode towards the bed without breaking stride. He dragged aside the crewel-work drape on the canopied four-poster and, pulling back the quilt, laid her down, lowering her head onto a pillow before he straightened up.

There was not a trace of the care of moments before in his actions as he began to tear off his clothes. As he fought his way out of them his eyes didn't leave hers for a moment.

He freed himself of the blue sweater and tossed it over his shoulder, still fumbling with the leather buckle at the waist of the kilt as he knelt beside her on the bed. The brass rings of the heavy drapes rattled as he pulled them closed behind him, leaving them cocooned inside the intimate velvet-lined tent.

In the enclosed space the scent of the lavender her grandmother lined the chest with where she stored her linen was stronger. The smell would for ever be associated with this moment in her mind. Every time her skirt brushed against a lavender bush she would think of Luca, think of the sheer, mind-numbing joy of reckless abandon.

Poppy, one hand thrown above her head, lay still, her eyes glued to the sleek hard lines of his bronzed torso, watching the play of muscle gliding under smooth skin. Her throat tightened and tears prickled the backs of her eyes as deep down inside her things shifted—he was so beautiful it hurt!

She had wanted this for so long!

Luca watched her, his eyes so dark and hot she couldn't breath. She could feel them burning a path over her skin through her clothes...*too many clothes.*

Maybe he read the thought or maybe he just knew what women wanted—either way he reached for the hem of her sweater and tugged it up her body and over her head.

'That looks a lot better on,' he said, looking at the tartan bra.

He slid a hand under her back and found the catch. *'Dio mio,'* he breathed reverently as her full breasts sprang free of their confinement. 'But I like this even better.'

He touched one rosy tipped peak and felt her gasp.

A predatory glow of satisfaction shone in his eyes. 'You're so sensitive,' he marvelled. 'Just relax, let me...'

Poppy opened her mouth to respond and forgot what

she was going to say, she forgot everything as he began to touch her, everywhere, his fingers and mouth gliding over her skin with a skill that awoke every single nerve ending in her body. And all the time he touched her she was aware deep down inside of something building, something dark and hot.

A little sliver of anxiety slid into her mind. He was so perfect—would he find her beautiful? She wanted to be beautiful for him.

He nuzzled her ear, kissing, his warm breath sending delicious shivers through her body as he whispered, 'Stop thinking, just feel, *cara*.'

The pleasure seemed almost too much to bear as his fingers trailed fire as they slid up the smooth skin of her inner thigh. It wasn't until his fingers moved higher into the heat and moisture of her arousal, parting the delicate folds to seek the throbbing nub, that she realised she was lying there totally naked.

When did that happen?

She smiled up at him and looked so wanton, sweet and almost shocked that he had to taste her. Gianluca brought his mouth down on hers and kissed her deeply as he fought to unfasten the buckle on the kilt.

Poppy kissed him back with a fierce hunger, her tongue against his tongue, their hot breaths and sighs mingling in a hoarse chorus of excitement.

'You're incredible...' Her passion and innate sensuality amazed and delighted him. Luca groaned when he was forced to reluctantly unwind her clinging arms from his neck.

'One second, *cara*,' he begged, kissing her hard before pulling back. 'I need both hands for this unless I am to maim myself.'

Poppy's indignant pout of protest faded when she saw what he was doing. She watched as he successfully relieved himself of the restriction of the folds of heavy tartan fabric.

As his erection sprang free and he knelt there naked and aroused she swallowed hard. Staring, she reached out, her fingers brushing the satiny tip before drawing back with a shocked gasp.

'You do this to me,' he said, taking her small hand and curving her fingers around the hard column.

Poppy felt him pulse against the pressure and gasped. 'Oh, God, you're—'

'Later,' he growled, taking her hand and placing it on the pillow beside her face, doing the same with the other before he began to kiss his way down her body... slowly tasting every inch of her.

Her skin burned where he touched, the pleasure came close to pain as Poppy bit her lip and gasped, her body arching as his hands caressed her thrusting breasts. When a moment later he lowered his body down onto hers the skin-to-skin contact sent a rush of pleasure through her body. Excited beyond bearing, she writhed beneath him, pushing up into his body, seeking to deepen the skin-to-skin contact.

The force of Luca's driving kiss pushed her head deep into the lavender-scented pillow.

They kissed for several frantic moments before he pulled back. He brushed the hair back from her hot cheek with one hand, watching her face as he slid his free hand between her legs, letting his fingers slide into the slick heat, hearing her gasp his name over and over before he reached for the condom and arranged himself between her thighs.

He heard her voice muffled against his neck murmur, *'I can do this,'* and paused. It sounded as though she was convincing herself.

'Has it been a long time?'

'Oh, yes, long…very long…'

'It'll be good…just relax…' Every sinew, every cell in his body ached with the driving need to possess her, it went bone deep, so strong he could taste it, but Luca fought the temptation to enter her in one powerful thrust. Instead he pushed slowly with infinite care a little at a time feeling her soften and tighten around him until she had almost taken him all, then he sighed and sank all the way.

She moaned his name and buried her face in his shoulder, her hands sliding over his sweat-slick shoulders before moving to his back.

How could she be that tight?

She jerked beneath him, her limbs plastic as he wrapped her long legs around his hips before repeating the process in reverse, pulling out and sinking back in, each time a little farther, each time a little harder.

The effort glossed his skin with perspiration that made it glow while beneath him Poppy, her eyes closed her lips parted, her face a mask of concentration, arched her back and clung, her fingernails digging into his shoulders. He used the pain, concentrating on it to help him cling to his control.

'Oh, Luca, that is so…you…I can't…' Poppy moaned and clung, letting herself move with the rhythm he had built. She could feel him everywhere, hot and hard, the sensual friction as he moved intensifying the wild excitement inside her. She felt so hot she was on fire. She had never imagined such pleasure existed.

Gianluca could feel her climax building. He let himself ride it with her, holding back, sharing the pleasure she was experiencing as the spasms and tremors of her body heightened his own pleasure to the point of pain.

He held on until her climax burst. He let her cry wash over him and felt her body tighten in a series of paroxysms of pleasure before he let himself go.

Panting, he rolled off her and removed the condom before rolling onto his back and waiting for his heart to slow.

Poppy turned her head on the pillow and forced her heavy eyelids apart. 'Thank you, that was…you are incredible…' She touched his sweat-slick chest, tangling her fingers in the damp hair. 'I never knew it would be so…'

Luca stiffened and knew…never knew because she never had.

How was it possible?

He covered her hand with his and rolled on his side, breathing hard. As he looked at her lying there, her hair spread out on the pillow around her face, the flush of desire still giving her skin an almost opalescent sheen, he waited for the guilt to hit. She had been a virgin and he had slept with her—he ought to feel guilty.

He didn't. He felt a fierce primitive satisfaction that incredibly he had after all been her first.

'So are you going to tell me how this is possible?' His bewilderment was genuine. Poppy was the most innately sensual creature he had ever encountered; it made no sense that she had never had a lover. Unless…?

The muscles along his jawline tightened as the idea took hold. 'Did you have a…bad experience?' The images that flashed through his head filled Luca with fury and a masculine frustration.

The object of his protective instincts remained utterly oblivious to his agony.

Poppy gave a luxuriant yawn and, stretching sinuously like a kitten, groaned. 'Do we have to talk about this?' Why spoil a perfect moment with explanations. Her brow puckered. 'Bad experience…what do you mean…?' Another yawn. 'Is it possible to be drunk without actually drinking alcohol?' She had never felt this high in her life. 'I wasn't very terrible, was I? No, that sounds needy. I was actually pretty great…I… Say something…'

A little of the tension left his face as he smiled. 'Yes, you were great.'

'I really wanted to lose it, you know.'

Luca inhaled deeply. 'When you commit to something you do it very wholeheartedly,' he breathed.

'It had become a real…nuisance.'

'Glad to be of help,' he murmured faintly. *Never expect Poppy to say what you expected.* He should not, he realized, have forgotten that.

'So it's all right with you if I just enjoy the moment… my first time, the only one I'll get to—'

Luca collapsed onto the bed laughing in defeat. 'All right, have your moment.'

'And you're not mad? Not that you have any right to be mad.'

'I'm not mad, I'm…blown away if you must know,' he growled.

'And the whole point of one-night stands is no talking, just wham bam and thank you—and I'm talking a lot—'

'This is not a one-night stand.'

Stroking his thigh, she missed the anger in his voice. 'What is it, then?'

'Unfinished business.'

She rolled onto her stomach and looked up at him. 'And now it's finished business?'

He curved a possessive hand over the soft curve of her bottom. His eyes glowed as if lit from within. 'I have barely started.'

She chewed her lip. 'That sounds interesting...' She was amazed at how easily the teasing came. How relaxed she felt, how natural... Could it have been this way with anyone but Luca?

The answer in her heart made her glad she had waited.

The corners of his incredible eyes crinkled in a way she found fascinating. 'I think I can do better than interesting.'

The arrogant boast made her smile. 'Talk is cheap,' she taunted.

He bent his head and kissed her hard and long enough for the heat to start building again, long enough for Poppy to lose any desire to talk.

CHAPTER SEVEN

THE next day dawned and a quick glance through the curtains confirmed that the storm still raged. The rain driven against the glass by a force-ten gale meant that she didn't have to think about what came next, she could just enjoy what came now.

And if it was anything like last night the now was going to be pretty incredible.

Poppy twitched the curtain back and, struggling to hide her delight, turned back to Luca, who lay stretched out on the bed, his eyes half closed, his glistening chest rising and falling rapidly.

She gave a voluptuous sigh of pleasure, her heartbeat louder just looking at him. She would never regret her decision. Luca had not been a good teacher, he had been *incredible*!

'It's still bad out there.' When there was no response she poked him in the ribs, drawing an indignant sleepy, *'Hey!'*

Luca opened one eye.

'You're so lazy!' she reproached.

'Me lazy!' he exclaimed. 'Easy for you to bounce around.' Bounce in every sense of the word, he thought as his eyes followed the undulations of her firm full breasts. 'I was the one doing all the work.'

She gave a sultry smile. 'I'm willing to give it a try if you want to lie back and think of Italy!'

His lean face split into a wide grin. 'You are a wicked woman, Poppy Ramsay.'

Poppy loved the sound of it... Wicked woman—it made her feel sexy and empowered. 'I'm trying,' she told him, her prim manner a stark contrast to her state of undress.

'I might die trying to keep up with you.'

She gave a chuckle. 'Oh, you do all right for an old man.'

Lucas sat up in bed. 'Who are you calling an old man?' His hand shot out without warning, his fingers curling around her ankle.

Poppy made a token struggle as he dragged her across the bed towards him until they both sat facing one another.

'What are you doing?'

Good question. The humour in his expression faded. 'You've got me there...'

Poppy shuffled in closer, wrapping her arms around his neck and pushing the coral tips of her breasts against his bare chest. 'God, this is perfect...you're perfect.' She felt him stiffen and pulled back a little to look him in the face.

'I am not perfect, Poppy.'

Luca was not aiming for perfection, he was aiming for getting through life without being the cause of serious casualties to innocent bystanders, which was why he surrounded himself with people as tough, selfish and self-centred as he was.

Poppy was soft, gentle, the total opposite.

The fact you did not *intentionally* set out to hurt someone was not in his opinion any mitigation. In fact not being conscious of how your actions might impact on others was an indictment in itself.

People he knew fooled themselves that they could change—become a *better* person. Gianluca had never bought into this self-delusional claptrap.

He did not believe in redemption; he did not believe that a person could change their personality—better to be aware of your own deficiencies, lead your life accordingly. He would never be a nice, caring, considerate person capable of putting others before himself, but he sure as hell would make sure he didn't destroy anyone else the way he had destroyed Aurelia.

An image of his dead wife's face floated through his head; shamefully her features were indistinct.

The warning in his voice was clear. Her lashes swept downwards. 'Poetic licence,' she said lightly.

'You do know that this is sex.' *What does she know about sex?* the voice in his head heckled. 'Don't fall in love with me, Poppy.'

His concern was not for himself, it was for Poppy. He had disconnected his emotions from the physical needs of his body a long time ago. It would take more than candles and a pair of big green eyes to change that, he told himself. He was in control of this situation.

As he spoke the self-deception she had worked so hard to maintain peeled away exposing the truth—she loved Luca. She had never stopped loving him; even while she had been hurting and hating him she had loved him.

She looked away for a moment and from somewhere found the strength to produce a smile and joke, 'I'll do my best—hard, of course, you being so irresistible...'

Some truths hurt more than others... Poppy wanted to lie in the dark alone to recover...a century might do the trick.

A shade of wariness remained in his eyes as he studied her face. Poppy reached up and brushed a hank of dark hair from his brow.

'Is it all right if I fall a little in lust, Luca?'

Poppy watched the wariness fade away as his eyes darkened dramatically. He grasped her hand and pressed his lips to the blue-veined inner aspect of her delicate wrist.

A hot charge scorched a path along the relevant nerve endings, dragging a shaky gasp from her throat.

Relieved that she had said something she was permitted to, Poppy told herself there was no harm in continuing to say what he wanted to hear, though for the duration the subject of *love* would remain a no-go area.

And the way she saw it, the longer this storm lasted, the more likely it was that Luca would see that he cared for her more than he was prepared to admit.

It might make her a hopeless optimist, or it might make her utterly deluded, but Poppy stubbornly refused to believe that anyone could make love with such exquisite tenderness and passion if their deeper emotions were not involved—just because things seemed unlikely didn't mean they didn't happen.

If anyone had told her this time a week ago that she would be living out her secret fantasy, that her first lover would be Luca, man, she would have laughed at them, but here she was.

Anything was possible.

CHAPTER EIGHT

It was midday when Poppy fell into a sleep of utter exhaustion; at that point they hadn't left the bed.

When she woke she lay there for a moment staring at the canopy overhead wondering where she was and why were muscles she didn't know she had hurting?

Then it all came flooding back.

With a gasp she turned her head to the pillow beside her—it was empty.

She might have thought she dreamt it all had it not been for the intimate aches. She reached out and felt the indentation where his body had been—it was still warm.

Almost fearfully she pulled aside the curtains. Her eyes went straight to the window. The sight of the storm-lashed landscape sent a rush of relief through her body as she flopped back with a sigh.

She knew that the reprieve was only temporary. The storm would end and they would leave...maybe bump into each other again in seven years' time. Luca might be married then, with a brood of children... He might not recognise her because she had taken up comfort eating and had several double chins.

Pushing aside this depressing image of the future—

a person didn't have to sit back and meekly accept their fate, did they?—she got out of bed, her jaw set at a determined angle. Meek was one thing she had never been accused of.

Then hurriedly—despite the fire burning cheerily it was freezing—she pulled on her clothes from the previous night.

Luca was breaking the seal on a bottle of whisky he had discovered when he heard a light footfall on the floor behind him.

From where he was sitting he could see the staircase and anyone on it. Poppy, he realized, must have used the narrow secondary staircase that came out in the boot room.

'Hello there, sleepy head,' he drawled, angling his head to see her approach reflected in the mirrored door of a lacquered Chinese cupboard that looked totally incongruous set against the rustic stone wall.

'Why didn't you wake me?' she grumbled.

Her big eyes looked back at him—well, not at him, at the back of his chair. They looked like dark mysterious shadows in her pale heart-shaped face.

Luca's mouth went dry and he felt a pressure in his chest. She was beautiful. Despite the fact they had spent the night and half the day in bed making love he wanted her. He saw her smile and he felt as if his heart would stop.

It was just sex.

Maybe, but it was the best sex he had ever had. No woman had ever responded with such uninhibited sensuality to him. Her vibrancy, her vitality, her earthy little laugh had bewitched him.

Poppy walked towards the sofa that Luca had pulled up to the fire. She could see the top of his dark head above the high back and his hand on the arm, the slim metal-banded watch he wore gleaming against his bronzed skin.

She shivered, feeling suddenly unaccountably shy as she moved forward. How could you be shy with someone who had pretty much explored every inch of your body?

Luca moved across the sofa to make room for her as she approached.

'What time is it?'

'Does it matter?'

She shrugged and sank down beside him on the saggy sofa, noticing his wet hair for the first time. 'Have you been outside?'

'Only to the log store.' He nodded towards the neat stack beside the inglenook. 'It's pretty wild out there.'

He surveyed her with hooded eyes and murmured, 'So were you.'

The colour flew to her face. 'I...I...' She finally bowed her head. 'Thank you,' she said, before experiencing a sudden flurry of insecurity and tacking on, 'I think...?'

Luca laughed, stopping when it occurred to him this was the most relaxed he had felt in a long time...sitting around doing nothing and relaxing. He had leisure time—a man needed balance in his life—but it never occurred to him to waste that time idly sitting by fires.

It had only taken the storm of the century to make him sit back and relax.

'You think right.'

Poppy relaxed slightly. 'You seem to have made yourself at home.' Her gesture took in the slab of cheese and the loaf of bread and packet of butter set on a wooden board. 'You never learnt to make a sandwich?'

'If pushed my culinary skills stretch that far, however the bread is not the freshest so I thought perhaps we could toast it?' He waved the toasting fork and nodded in the direction of the leaping flames. 'You used to like that?'

'I did. This is nice, Luca.' It was heaven.

'Are you hungry?'

'Yes!' Actually ravenous would be a more accurate description. 'So have you been awake long?'

'A while. I have been going through some of Aunt Isabel's correspondence and what an interesting filing system she has,' he added, nodding towards papers and then the plastic carrier bags he had already been sifting through. There were an equal number he had not yet begun to sort. 'She hadn't even opened most of the letters from the council.' He found such an attitude hard to comprehend.

'I think she burnt a lot of the early ones,' Poppy admitted unhappily. 'If only she'd said something sooner. My dad gave me the name of a solicitor. I suppose you know lawyers?'

'A few,' he admitted, thinking of his highly qualified and overpaid legal department who would drop everything at a word from him. 'And if necessary I will call in the big guns, but from what I have read I think we should be able to handle this.'

'So how long will that take, do you think?'

'It's hard to tell, but don't worry—I love this place. I'll make sure she doesn't lose it.'

Poppy looked at him curiously. 'I always wondered,

Luca, didn't your parents ever mind you spending the summers here?' At the time she had never questioned his presence, just taking it for granted.

'My father travelled a lot with work and my mother always went with him on all his business trips. By the time I was ten the novelty of being able to order what I liked from room service had worn off. I think they were relieved when what had been intended to be a one-off became a custom.

'Have a drink.'

Poppy looked from the glass in his hand to him and shook her head.

'Don't worry, I'm not trying to get you drunk.'

'You don't need to,' she told him bluntly. Presumably she was not telling him anything he didn't already know. Not that he had even tried to kiss her yet...

Should she take the initiative?

'I don't actually like whisky,' she admitted.

His brows lifted. 'This is a twenty-year-old malt.'

His unfeigned horror made Poppy's lips twitch. 'Is that good?' she wondered with a pretended innocence.

It might be a taste she had never acquired but there wasn't actually much Poppy didn't know about whisky, after being dragged around tours of most of the distilleries in the country by her father.

He laughed and allowed his gaze to linger on her soft lips. 'And you half Scottish—it's sacrilege.'

Poppy rolled her eyes. 'So hang me.'

'I'd prefer to—' He bent forward and fitted his mouth to hers. The moment of contact Poppy just went up in flames. 'That,' he completed some time later.

Poppy gave a dazed nod and unfurled her clenched fingers from the front of his sweater. Her dilated darkened eyes on his face with unconcealed longing, she struggled for breath.

They sat there staring hungrily at one another until Luca said, 'You need to eat first.'

Her eyes widened in protest. 'But!'

He was tempted, then he remembered the moment last night when she had terrified him by appearing to lose consciousness for a moment in the height of passion and firmed his resolve. 'Eat first.'

Poppy didn't ask what came after, she knew, and her body ached for it. 'Hold on…'

'Where are you going?'

'Hold on, Gran usually keeps a…'

Gianluca watched her run across the room. The grace and fluidity of her impetuous dash reminded him of a dancer, one of those fey creatures with the big eyes in the Degas painting.

She reached a large ugly bureau and stopped and, dropping to her knees, opened one of the doors and peered through the accumulated junk—Gran never threw anything away on the principle it might one day be *handy*.

'I *thought* she kept some here.'

Gianluca had adjusted his position automatically so that he could get a better view of her delicious bottom, then, realising what he was doing, he leaned back in his seat with a scowl. He was acting like a schoolboy.

'There should be, yes.' Poppy gave a triumphant grunt as she extracted a dusty bottle from the back of the cupboard and waved it above her head. Going to the drawer above, she located the corkscrew and shoved it in the pocket of her jeans. Popping a stack of paper cups from the cupboard on top of the bottle, she tucked it under her arm before returning to the fire, pausing along the way to grab a few cushions off a chair.

'That is wine?' Gianluca asked, eyeing the bottle clutched triumphantly to her bosom with some suspicion.

'Gran's home-made wine.' She read the handwritten label on the bottle out loud. 'Blackberry, great—that's almost as good as her parsnip,' she enthused.

Gianluca studied her face. *Dio*, but she was serious. 'Wow, this is our lucky day.'

She heard the sarcasm. 'God, a wine snob...' She artfully stifled a fake yawn.

'I prefer my wine less vegetable based,' he admitted. 'And paper cups...?' His pained glance took in the flimsy carton she clutched.

'It saves on washing up.'

'So does eating with your fingers.'

'I never eat fish and chips any other way.' Her glance lingering on the firm contours of his wide mobile mouth, she dropped the cushions on the floor in front of the fire and took up a graceful cross-legged pose on them, displaying the sort of elasticity that had delighted him in the bedroom.

'The having-women-worship-at-my-feet thing just never gets old.'

Poppy stole a look at him through her eyelashes— on the gorgeous and sexy scale he was off the chart. 'In your dreams.'

Gianluca acknowledged her mutter with a lopsided, wildly attractive grin and picked up the toasting fork.

'Ladies first,' he said, handing it to her.

'Always the gentleman,' she murmured, not quite meeting his eyes as she took it off him.

She was very hungry.

Finally replete, Poppy put the toasting fork on the hearth and settled back on the cushions she had arranged on the floor in front of the crackling fire. She lifted a hand to touch the cheek turned to the fire—a tactical retreat seemed called for unless she wanted to roast.

'What are you doing?' She reminded him of a cat finding a comfortable spot to sleep in.

'I'm turning around—this side of my face is burning,' she said, pointing to the cheek in question.

'So you are going to roast the other to even things up. It's a plan,' he admitted, amused. 'Or you could always sit up here.'

Poppy gave a slow smile and flashed him a challenging look from under the sweep of her lashes. 'Want to come get me?'

'I might be persuaded,' he agreed, watching through narrowed eyes as she licked the butter off her fingers before angling her head towards the flame, shaking out her loose hair and tilting her head to free the strands that had become trapped in the neck of her sweater. The waves fell over her shoulder and down her slender back, the flames turning the paler highlights to rich polished gold.

The unstudied sensuality of her actions sent a lick of fresh lust through his body like a forest fire, raising his core temperature by several degrees. He only realised that he was almost panting when he saw the mist on the glass he had raised to his lips.

He took a long swallow and put it down hard enough to make some of the twenty-year-old malt slop over onto the table.

Maybe it was the isolation factor or maybe there was something in the water, but he just couldn't get enough of her.

He reached out a hand and she took it, allowing him to tug her to her feet. Instead of taking the seat beside him, she positioned herself on his lap, facing him, her knees either side of his thighs as she shuffled in closer.

'It's a pity that your jeans have dried,' she mused with regret as she ran her spread palms slowly up the iron-hard contours of his thighs.

Luca shifted in his seat and swallowed.

'I liked the kilt. Mind you, there's nowhere for you to hide in these, is there?' she mused, running one finger across the swelling bulge of his rock-hard erection.

'P-Poppy!'

She gave a slow sensual smile and adopted an innocent expression. 'Is there a problem?'

He grinned back. 'Nothing I can't handle.'

Poppy let out a startled shriek as she found herself tipped backwards then, without quite knowing how, she found herself lying flat on her back among the tumbled cushions.

Luca was kneeling straddled across her like some pagan god, his dark gleaming eyes holding hers as he slowly slipped the buckle on his belt. She licked her dry lips, her heart thudding in anticipation.

'You have no idea at all, do you?' he slurred. 'What you do to a man.'

'Tell me.'

'I'm more an actions-speak-louder-than-words type

of guy and at this moment I'm in a kind of...on-top mood. If that's all right with you?'

Poppy reached up to assist him with the recalcitrant jeans murmuring a fervent, 'Very all right.'

CHAPTER NINE

WHEN Luca decided an hour or so later that they should transfer back to bed Poppy pointed out they had only recently left it.

'We can't just stay in bed all day,' she felt obliged to protest.

Luca retrieved his sweater from the corner where it had landed and fought his way into it, it took him longer to put it on than it had taken to remove it. 'Why?' he asked as he opened a folded throw and draped it across her bare shoulders.

'Well, it's…'

He raised a brow.

'Well, people just don't,' she finished lamely. She was just going through the motions with her protest and they both knew. 'And I don't even know what time it is.'

And if he started to kiss her she wouldn't even know what her name was or where she began and he ended… Luca was in her bloodstream like a narcotic and she was well and truly hooked.

Poppy hardly recognised herself. In the space of twenty-four hours she had morphed from a wary virgin into some sex-crazed vamp who could not keep her hands off Luca. She had done things that she would have previously considered shocking and not felt even slightly shocked.

'Here.' He slid the metal-banded watch over his hand and onto hers. It hung loose around her delicate narrow wrist. 'Now you will always know what time it is in several time zones and also you can dive.'

'Yes, that's going to be incredibly useful,' she remarked drily as she held up her wrist to stop it sliding off.

'You might not have noticed but the temperature has dropped by several degrees and, though it pains me to say this—' his dark hooded glance made an appreciative sweep over the delicious contours of her firm body '—you really ought to get dressed.'

On cue Poppy shivered. 'Where are my clothes?'

Luca handed her the pink sweater. 'I think you could actually fly a kite in here.' He glanced towards the section of broken windows.

'Where's my bra?'

He shrugged and she pulled the sweater over her head with an exasperated grunt.

'The point is this room is impossible to heat. We could shift to the kitchen but the seating arrangement is a little basic for my taste. The suggestion to move to the bedroom is purely practical. I'm not inviting you to an orgy, though that is of course available on request— all you have to do is ask.'

'And what makes you think I won't?' Shocked by her boldness, she gave a small laugh. Only yesterday his comment would have covered her in confusion.

Luca laughed too, a deep, delicious, throaty sound,

then stopped, his expression becoming quizzical as he tipped his head to one side in a listening attitude.

'Did you hear that?' He glanced back at her eyes, narrowed.

Poppy shrugged and pulled her hair from the neck of her sweater before pushing it back with both hands from her face. 'What?' All she could hear was the wind and rain.

He shook his head in dismissal before continuing, 'I just thought that the bedroom seems a more comfortable arrangement. But it is your choice.'

'The bedroom sounds good,' she admitted, pulling her jeans over her slim hips. Her socks and bra appeared to have totally disappeared. 'Are you listening to me?'

'There it is again.' The indent above his masterful nose deepened.

Poppy listened, then shook her head. 'I don't hear anything. I can only find one sock,' she complained, holding it up.

'I'm going to check it out.'

Her head came up with a jerk. 'No!'

His startled eyes zeroed in on her face.

Poppy shook her head. 'You can't go out, it's awful...'

'I'm not afraid of the rain.'

'That's the problem!'

He elevated a brow and looked amused. 'You want me to be afraid of the rain.'

'It's not a joke, Luca. You're not afraid of anything,' she accused bitterly. 'And you think you're invulnerable, that makes you do s-stupid things.' If anything happened to him she could literally not bear it.

'Relax, I'm just going outside...nothing is going to happen,' he soothed, sounding amused.

'Oh, you're psychic now too, are you?' Her fingernails bit half-moons in her palms as she levelled a frustrated glare at his face. 'Or have you come to some sort
of agreement with the roof slates and they've agreed not
to fall off while you're wandering around?'

Luca shook his head and laid a hand on her forehead.
'No temperature.'

Poppy shrugged him away with an angry snort.

'You're wildly overreacting here, *cara*.'

'I am not overreacting...' She stopped; this time she
heard the cry too. 'I'm coming with you,' she decided.
Going with him was to her way of thinking infinitely
preferable to sitting here waiting for his return.

'No, you are not.'

She glared at him. 'No...?'

They argued back and forth and somehow, she
was not quite sure how, Luca won and Poppy was left
alone to pace the floor while she waited for his return.
Tortured by a succession of vivid nightmare images
of him lying crushed and broken. She would give him
five minutes...five, then that was it, she was going out
there!

She didn't have to—before the time was up the door
swung open and a wet and windblown Luca stepped in
along with assorted storm debris that blew in with him.

Poppy rushed to close the door behind him.

'Did you see anything?' She stopped, noticing for
the first time that instead of wearing the heavy army
surplus greatcoat she had found in the boot room and
made him wear, he was carrying it in his arms.

Before she could ask him why it had seemed a good
idea to strip off outside he laid the coat on the floor...
It moved.

'What—? Oh, my gosh, it's a cat!' Poppy exclaimed as a small head poked out. The bedraggled creature let out a pitiful cry. 'Oh, you poor sweet thing.'

Before he could react Poppy was on her knees beside the animal. Luca started forward, arm outstretched. 'No, don't touch, it's...' he began, then stopped, shaking his head ruefully as the spitting bundle of fury that had scratched him by way of gratitude began to purr as Poppy stroked its mangy head. 'Vicious,' he finished drily.

'Where did you find it?'

'It had got locked in the log store.'

'Goodness it must be terrified. Were you scared, sweetheart? And hungry.'

Luca was sent to the pantry to find food and milk while the animal, who clearly knew a soft touch when it saw one, continued to worm its way into Poppy's affection.

Poppy stood beside him and watched as the animal wolfed down a plate of canned salmon and drank a bowl of milk dry.

'The poor little thing—she was starving. I wonder where she comes from. Is someone missing you...?'

He elevated a dark brow. 'Are you talking to me, or the cat?'

Poppy tossed him an amused look over her shoulder. 'Anyone would think you were jealous,' she teased.

His brows lifted. 'Well, I'd ask you to choose but I know I'd lose out.' The day had come when he was jealous of a cat! Or at least the stroking attention it was receiving.

'It'll have to come upstairs with us.'

'That revolting thing?' he exclaimed, shaking his head. 'It probably has fleas.'

Poppy sent him a look of reproach and touched a finger to her lips. 'Hush, she'll hear you.'

'You are afraid I'll hurt its feelings? That cat is not coming upstairs, Poppy. Don't look at me like that. I'm not asking you to throw her back out—the kitchen is warm.' And it was the place for animals.

One look at the tilt of her chin and it was an argument he was resigned to lose.

He did.

Ten minutes later Luca found himself carrying the cat wrapped in a blanket up the stairs.

The purring animal got settled beside the fire and was fussed over by Poppy until Luca growled.

'You're pushing it!' And he picked Poppy up.

She complained loudly as she was dumped on the bed, but in reality she was only mildly indignant at the treatment.

'You're a hard man!' she accused, thinking, *And in all the right places.*

She put a pillow behind her head and watched as he threw some more logs on the fire, loving the way he moved, loving everything about him.

God, I really am living my fantasy!

Please let the storm last!

The wish made her feel instantly guilty. While the storm lasted her family had no way of knowing where she was and if she was safe—they'd be worried sick and she hadn't given them a thought.

She shook her head. 'He'll be frantic.'

Luca, in the act of lighting the candles in the window, turned his head. 'Who?'

'My dad. He'll feel guilty because he let me come here alone.'

'Why did he?'

'He and Gran...'

Luca gave a murmur of amazement; he recalled the family rift but not the reason for it. 'Surely he and your grandmother have resolved their differences by now?'

Poppy threw up her hands in a gesture of exasperation. 'You assumed, Luca, that they've got a grain of sense between them. Big mistake. He's as stubborn as Gran is and neither of them will give an inch. Since he remarried he and Gran have hardly spoken. She doesn't approve of Millie.'

'But you still get on with your stepmother?'

Poppy's expression softened. 'She's a darling and she makes Dad so happy.'

'But not Isabel?'

Poppy expelled a rueful sigh and shook her head. 'It's so silly. Millie is great but, according to Gran, a housekeeper is not good enough for Dad.' She rolled her eyes. 'Her uncle's not an earl.'

'Not many people have uncles who are earls.'

'Mum did.'

'Ah...' Gianluca was seeing the light.

'The fact is Millie is the best thing that could have happened to Dad after—Mum. It's totally crazy but even after everything Mum did—does—as far as Gran is concerned her blue blood makes her a tough act to follow... I'm afraid she's a terrible snob,' Poppy confided ruefully. 'And so stubborn once she'd dug her heels in, and she did. She said he had to choose, so obviously he chose Millie, and I think Gran regrets laying down an ultimatum but she won't back down...'

'And you are stuck in the middle.'

Poppy nodded. 'I hate it,' she confided. 'God, I'm sorry—this family stuff must be boring you to death.' She slanted an uneasy look towards Luca.

'I will tell you if I'm bored.'

A little laugh was drawn from Poppy's throat. 'I suppose you would.'

For a nerve-splitting moment their eyes connected. The sardonic amusement in Gianluca's faded, leaving in its place a fierce driven expression that made Poppy's traitorous heart skip a beat.

He has to love me!

'S-sometimes...' She paused, cleared her throat and started again, wrenching her eyes free of his as she began to speak. 'Sometimes I think I should just invite them both to my flat and lock them in until they sort out their differences...'

A laugh drew her questioning eyes back to his face. 'A bit like this?'

'Not at all like this! This is a castle—there's plenty of room to escape if we wanted to.'

'But we don't want to?'

She nodded her head in agreement. 'And we have nothing to resolve...' Poppy swallowed her disappointment when he didn't respond to her unspoken question—maybe she was being too subtle. 'The irony is if Gran got to know Millie she'd love her. Everyone does—she's sweet and loyal and kind, the total opposite of my mother.'

'Do you ever see her, your mother?' Lady Maria Cunningham was a woman that the terms 'sweet' and 'loyal' were never going to be used in connection with, Gianluca mused wryly.

Millie shook her head. 'Not really,' she admitted.

Despite this lack of contact, the news that she was that Lady Maria's daughter had somehow got out at the girls' school she had attended. After that there was rarely a week when a picture of her mother torn out of a tabloid or celebrity magazine wouldn't appear on the notice board with the word 'Slag' written across it in red felt pen. She could always hear the giggles when she ripped them down, knowing as she did so that they would appear somewhere else in the school.

Defending her mum's honour had earned her detention on more than one occasion.

'I get birthday presents and she usually invites me...' She stopped, adding with a self-conscious grimace, 'To her weddings.' Millie did a quick mental calculation. 'Five to date.'

'Did you go to any?' Gianluca asked. He could not recall seeing her at either of the two he had attended, the last being to her present husband, an Italian industrialist that his family had links with.

Poppy shook her head. 'She was only being polite. When I was little I might have got her dress dirty, when I got older I was not...as you know, cute-looking and now—'

'You'd be competition,' he completed.

Maria was far too media savvy to risk being photographed next to her beautiful daughter, having people remark on the contrast between Poppy's fresh-faced, vibrant beauty and her own more mature appearance. Not that Poppy's mother was not still a beautiful woman— though in Gianluca's mind she would have looked better had her search for perpetual youth not led her to smooth out any suggestion of a character line on her face—but she was not the type who liked competition.

'Hardly!' She laughed. 'She's beautiful.' While Poppy knew she was perfectly OK to look at she knew she was not, and never would be, in her mother's league.

'You actually look a lot like her.'

Poppy was startled by his assessment and uncomfortable by his prolonged scrutiny.

'Without the hard edges.' And with an innate sensuality that even with all the cosmetic procedures in the world her parent would never have. He would previously have laughed at anyone who used the phrase inner glow…but it was true and Poppy was the living, breathing proof.

'I look nothing like her!' Poppy protested, while in the back of her head a voice said, *He thinks you're beautiful.* 'She's—'

'A hard, selfish self-publicist with zero maternal instincts.'

Poppy's chin lifted. 'That's my mother you're talking about.'

'I know—tough gig,' he drawled sympathetically.

Poppy levelled a rebellious look at him as he joined her on the bed. 'I know people think a woman who leaves her child is terrible…and, all right, it's something I don't really understand.' The thought of deserting a child—any child, but her own flesh and blood… The concept was one that Poppy struggled with. She knew she would fight like a tigress if anyone tried to take her child from her.

'But I think it was a good thing for me she left… If she'd stayed she'd have been unhappy and resented, but she left and I got Millie.' Poppy had kept track of her mother's progress along with every other reader of gossip columns. The public had an apparently endless appetite for tales of the wild exploits of the titled English rose and her succession of rich husbands and lovers.

Occasionally when her husbands were listed she and George got mentioned as the children of marriages number one and three. Except on the memorable occasion when their mother, who was not good with names, had called them her two little accidents during a TV interview.

A sudden awful thought occurred to her. 'God, you haven't slept with her, have you?'

'Slept with who?'

'My mother.'

A choking sound left Luca's throat. 'No, I have not slept with your mother!' He had been propositioned on one occasion but he saw no need to share this information.

'I just thought...you are exactly the sort of man she likes and Jack, number three, was actually younger than you. I've not offended you, have I?'

'No, you have not offended me.'

'I used to think that it was my fault Mum left,' she heard herself admit. 'George felt the same.'

Gianluca's dark brows twitched into a line above his masterful nose. 'George?'

'My half-brother. His dad was the film director so George had therapy and I had Millie. We both grew up relatively normal.'

'You do know that you are almost too balanced to be true...?'

Poppy gave an embarrassed shrug and tucked her

feet under the quilt. 'Twenty-five-year-old virgin, re-member…?'

An expression she struggled to interpret moved at the back of his eyes. 'I have not forgotten. You must have had boyfriends…?' He saw her expression and said, 'One particular boyfriend?' The theory that someone had hurt her had not gone away.

'I've had a lot of boyfriends but none that I…' She stopped and thought, *None that were you.* 'The last one was actually a bit of a disaster.'

He arched a brow. 'How so?'

'You'll laugh, I know, but it turned out that he dated me for a bet. There were actually odds on whether I was a virgin and if I was who would be first to…you know.'

Gianluca did not laugh.

With a sudden explosive motion he surged to his feet, causing the cat to scuttle under a dressing table.

He stood there looking impossibly tall, imposing and terrifying and loosed a volley of violent-sounding oaths in his native tongue.

'You don't have to say it. I know I was stupid.'

He dragged a hand through his dark hair and laughed. '*You* were stupid?'

With no physical outlet for the outrage that pounded through his veins, short of battering a hole through the stone wall with his fists, it was a while before Gianluca trusted himself to speak.

'And you found out about this…*bet* how?'

Poppy couldn't take her eyes off the muscle that throbbed in his lean cheek, slowly clenching and un-clenching. His entire body was vibrating with anger; he looked pretty magnificent mad, and also quite scary.

'Rupert sent an email. It was meant for a few of

his mates only the entire building received it, including me.'

She paused and swallowed. It had not been the best day of her life. 'It pretty much said that he was about to win his bet and be the first to...' Unable to repeat the crude phrase he had used, she shook her head and said, 'You know?'

Gianluca did know.

He knew that if the pathetic loser had been within choking distance at that moment he would have taken great satisfaction from throttling him.

'I am assuming these men were disciplined?' If it had been his firm they would have been out on their ears.

'Rupert got his wrists slapped.'

'Wrists slapped?' he echoed incredulously.

'It didn't really matter because I had handed in my notice by then.'

Actually they had not made her work it, and she had taken advantage of the generosity but not the offer of the very healthy severance cheque, explaining to the startled-looking man in Human Resources that she didn't need money to keep her mouth closed because the last thing she wanted was this story making it outside the building.

He had almost fallen over himself assuring her that the severance cheque came with no strings, it was simply an acknowledgement of the excellent work she had done.

Poppy tilted her head back and made herself meet Gianluca's eyes.

'I know you think I overreacted, and maybe I could have handled it better, just kept my head down and waited for the dust to settle. But I never really felt comfortable there—it was all a bit…anonymous for me. I was much happier in my previous job where I knew everyone…but when they folded…' She gave a shrug. At the time she had been excited at getting the job in the high-powered firm. In an economic climate when there were so many well-qualified candidates scrabbling for a limited number of vacancies, Poppy had thought herself one of the lucky ones.

'So essentially you are the victim of this workplace harassment and *you* end up without a job…' He shook his dark head and thundered, 'This is insupportable!'

'But it all worked out for the best because Phil—'

She blinked as he bit out another violent-sounding oath. Icily outraged now, he pinned her with a stare like a surgical blade. 'You are missing the point.'

'No, I'm not missing the point, Gianluca!' she yelled back. 'Do you really think I don't know what *should* have happened? The point is it didn't and it never was going to, and, yes, maybe if I was a braver person I would have stayed and defended a principle, but I'm not brave—

'I ran because even if I'd got Rupert suspended—which, for the record, was never going to happen as his uncle is the CEO—I would always be *the virgin!*' Her narrow shoulders slumped. 'The joke. It's the noticeboard thing all over again,' she concluded dully.

The permanent groove above his masterful nose deepened. 'Notice board…?'

'It doesn't matter,' she said wearily. 'It was a school thing…at least this is not going to happen again.'

'You think the attitude will change at this place you worked?'

Poppy knew she should care for the sake of other

women, but she didn't. This was personal and it was time she took some positive action and thought about number one.

'No, *I've* changed. I'm not a...'

His expression froze. 'And that was the plan, was it...? Is that what this is about?' His stabbing gesture took in the tumbled bed sheets.

'What this?'

'Is that why you slept with me?'

CHAPTER TEN

'WHAT?' Poppy shook her head, confused by his accusing manner and the sudden hostility he was vibrating with.

'You heard me,' he gritted grimly. *'You used me!'* Luca stopped dead, recognising the utter absurdity of the accusation the moment it left his lips... *Used...?* He was the user the taker... Poppy had given him a gift. The problem was he wasn't worthy of it.

Poppy's jaw dropped at this take on the situation. 'I...' She began laughing. 'I suppose I did.'

Luca clenched his teeth, the dark lines of mortified colour scoring his cheekbones deepening.

'What do you want me to say, Luca—that I slept with you because I am madly in love with you?'

Luca, in the act of pacing to the window, stopped dead.

'Oh, I forgot, that isn't allowed either, is it? What— do you think I arranged for the storm? I arranged for you to get yourself shipwrecked...? It wasn't planned, it just happened and, yes, I did want to lose my virginity... Why is that suddenly a crime? Or is this about your high moral standards?' she continued in the same reasonable voice. 'You only have one-night stands with women who are *not* screwed-up virgins?

'But actually I'm not—if anyone is screwed up here, it's you!'

Gianluca glared at her. My God, she was right!

'What are you doing?' she asked, panic in her voice as he began to stride towards the door. 'Are you leaving…?' He didn't reply, but the sound of the door slamming was pretty eloquent.

Poppy flopped back on the bed. 'Well, at least there are plenty of spare rooms for him to choose from.'

Nursing her anger, and the cat that crept onto the bed, Poppy held out until three in the morning—according to Luca's watch.

She sat up in bed and pushed her tumbled curls from her face. 'What are you doing, Poppy?' They might only have a few more hours and she was wasting those precious moments waiting for him to apologise—as if it mattered!

'Idiot! No, not you, puss,' she said, scooping the cat off the bed and returning her to the makeshift bed by the fire. 'Sorry, but that place is already taken.'

She took a deep breath, lifted her chin and, candle in hand, she crept along the cold corridor, heading towards the light at the bottom of the stairs.

He was considering leaving his chair when he heard the sound of muffled footsteps. Struggling to locate the direction, he glanced at the clock on the wall, an item like many in the room that would have been labelled fifties kitsch nowadays and cost a fortune.

As he registered that it was three a.m. the door swung inwards with a creak and Poppy, her glorious hair tousled, her eyes heavy and blurry with sleep, or the lack of it, walked into the room. The thick woollen socks on her small feet explained the muffled sound of her approach.

'Luca...?' She had hardly said his name when he was there in front of her, towering over her.

Her heart thudding, her gaze made a slow journey up the length of his body, her head tilting backwards to look into his face. The febrile glow in his deep set dark eyes made her dizzy and set the butterflies in her belly into a painful frenzy of activity.

'Will you come back to bed?'

'Will I...?' He gave a strange laugh. 'You have no idea at all,' he slurred, framing her face with the long brown fingers of one hand while he planted the thumb of the free hand under her chin.

Poppy's knees gave and she grabbed the first thing that came to hand—his sweater. 'About what?' she whispered.

One hand slid to the base of her spine, his long fingers splaying across the curve of her bottom. 'This,' he said, hauling her body into his as he lowered his head and covered her soft mouth.

Poppy melted, her body moulding to his hard male frame, excited beyond belief by the raw hunger in his kiss as she kissed him back with a feverish desperation, her hands sliding under his sweater and over the smooth silky skin of his back.

Gianluca's groan was lost inside her mouth as, with his mouth still connected to hers and half carrying her, he backed her into the wall.

Poppy was dimly conscious of the cold roughness

of stone against her back as she continued to kiss him, stopping only to gasp, 'Oh, God!' when she felt the brazen thrust of his erection as it ground into the softness of her belly. 'Please...yes...you're...'

Breathing hard, his glittering gaze glued to her flushed face, he reached out to push the door open.

Poppy shook her head; she could hardly breathe. 'No...I can't wait...here now...I need...'

His nostrils flared. 'Now...?'

She nodded, breathing as hard now as he was.

Both her hands grasped in one of his, he lifted them above her head. With his free hand he caressed her body until she gasped and pleaded.

The sound of his zip was loud. Poppy could feel the tremors running through his body as he pressed her against the wall, their bodies sealed at waist level.

Holding her eyes, Luca wrapped his arm around her waist and lifted her off the ground then in one smooth motion slammed up and into her.

After the frantic coupling was over Poppy would have slid to the floor had it not been for the arm still banded around her middle.

Her eyes were closed as he swept her up into his arms and carried her back up the stairs.

Back in bed, he removed her clothes, then his, and got in beside her. She shivered as his warm skin touched her own.

'The things I do with you...I never imagined, Luca,' she whispered.

He kissed her with a tenderness that brought tears to her eyes. *'Piccola mia,'* he murmured.

'I can't keep my eyes open.'

'Don't try.'

Like a kitten she was asleep in seconds. Luca lay awake watching her sleep, not moving for fear of disturbing her, not even when the moth-eaten cat came to sleep on his feet.

She woke alone, but it was not Luca's absence that struck her—there was something else... Then it hit her: the silence.

It was over.

The bathroom when she got there showed signs of recent use but...no message on the mirror. She blinked to hold back the sudden rush of tears.

When she got to the kitchen Luca was standing staring out of the window. He turned his head when she walked in.

'I wondered where she was,' she said, looking at the cat that curled around his ankles. 'She likes you.'

'That's the food I gave her.'

'The wind has dropped,' she said brightly.

'So it has.'

'And it's stopped raining.' He was treating her like a stranger almost and after last night...?

Come out of your fantasy world, Poppy, she told herself. *Last night was* just sex... She could almost hear him saying it.

'Yes.' He rubbed a hand across the dark growth on his jaw. The dark shadow was a lot more defined this morning. Along with his heavy eyes it gave him an air of dangerous dissipation that was extremely sexy.

'Have you tried the phones yet?'

He shook his head.

'It's stopped raining.'

His brows lifted. 'So you mentioned. The weather seems to have affected your mood.'

She gave a light laugh. 'I do not do conversation until after my second cup of coffee.'

'There's no coffee.'

'Your point being?' She lowered her gaze and exhaled. 'This is it, then.'

He turned back to the window. 'It is what?'

'Goodbye.' She was filled with admiration for her calm delivery. 'I expect someone will be here soon, we're rescued...back to the real world—electricity, clean clothes, phones...civilisation.' The wrench of yearning she felt as she looked at him made her feel physically sick.

A nerve clenched in his jaw as he turned to look at her. 'It does not have to be...?'

'Be what?'

'Goodbye.'

Her heart began to thud in response to the enigmatic response. 'So what exactly are you saying, Luca?'

'I'll be staying around until Aunt Isabel's affairs are sorted and I'm assuming you...?' He arched a brow and she nodded. 'We could meet up...?'

Poppy's expression froze. 'Have sex, you mean?'

His jaw clenched. 'Yes, have sex.'

'Yes!' she blurted. She looked away, biting her lip and wishing she had at least pretended to consider it.

'Good. Then that is settled.'

He made it sound simple but Poppy knew it was not. Having a wild passionate affair in an isolated castle was one thing... 'God knows what Gran will say...'

'There is no need for Aunt Isabel to say anything.

With a little discretion there is no need for anyone to know.'

'A secret, you mean.'

'I like to keep my personal life just that.'

'And I suppose if anyone realised you were sleeping with Maria Cunningham's daughter…'

Her ready understanding of the situation was a relief. 'The press would have a field day.' He shuddered at the thought of her being pursued by tacky tabloids. It was something he was determined to protect Poppy from.

'And I don't suppose that your family would be too happy either…'

'What has it got to do with—?'

'Poppy, lass, am I glad to see you!'

They both turned to see a big red-headed man in a bright red waterproof standing framed in the doorway, beaming from ear to ear as he lifted a mobile phone to his ear and yelled.

'Yes, Uncle Fergus, she's here and she's safe and sound and it looks like the daft Italian bloke who bought the boat isn't dead. Yeah, he's here large as life, aye… aye, I will.' Still smiling, he slid the phone back into his pocket and explained rather unnecessarily, 'That was Uncle Fergus.'

Poppy slid a surreptitious glance towards Luca to see how he was coping with being referred to as the *daft Italian* and found that he was not looking at Dougal but at her, his dark intense stare aimed directly at her face. She looked away quickly but not before he sent a deep shiver through her body.

'Your gran and Uncle Fergus—they were all really worried about you when they heard that idiot had ferried you out here and left you. But not to worry—I'm here now and there's no need to cry, lass.'

'I'm not crying,' Poppy said, wiping a hand across her damp face.

'Any chance of a cuppa?'

Poppy laughed and said, 'Definitely. I really can't tell you how glad I am to see you.' A sliver of the anxiety she had never quite managed to totally rid herself of appeared in her eyes as she tacked on, 'Gran—is she...?'

'Och, she's fine, or she will be now she knows you're all right.' Unzipping his waterproof, he walked over to Gianluca, his hand outstretched. 'Dougal.'

Gianluca allowed his hand to be briefly clasped in the beefy grip.

'Gianluca Ranieri.'

'I'm thinking there are going to be a few people happy to see you, Mr Ranieri. I must say you look pretty fit for a dead man.'

'A dead man?' Gianluca echoed, only half his attention on what the other man was saying. Most of his mind was focused on the slim figure in the periphery of his vision. Their unfinished conversation frustrated him.

'Aye, they found the boat, or what remained of it. The coastguard hasn't called off the search yet but, I have to tell you, they don't really expect to find anyone alive.'

'As you see, I am.' Gianluca's agile mind began to assess the implications of this information. Hopefully the news of his demise had not spread beyond the locality—if so the financial markets would not have been affected.

The cheery Scotsman's next words dashed this hope.

'There are television cameras all over the place,

not just the BBC—from all over and foreigners too. The bars are doing a roaring trade. You must be famous. God, wait until they find out you're not dead!' He chuckled, clearly amused by the prospect.

Gianluca felt less inclined to laugh over the thought of a media scrum. This was going to make concealing an affair with Poppy even tougher.

'And when they see you getting off the boat with the lovely Poppy here...' He released a silent whistle and directed what Gianluca judged to be a lecherous leer Poppy's way. 'I hope you've no jealous lady at home.'

'I think it would be better all round, Dougal, if you took Mr Ranieri back first and come back for me, if that's no problem for you?'

Gianluca flashed her a look. 'Thank you for your input, *Miss* Ramsay, but—'

He stopped, a mental image of Poppy walking straight into the eye of a media storm flashing before his eyes.

She wouldn't know what had hit her.

'That is an excellent idea,' he finished smoothly.

'No problem,' Poppy said with a shrug. She had offered so it was irrational to feel piqued by his ready agreement to the scheme.

Why would he object? He wanted to keep things secret. He didn't want the world to know he'd been stranded in a Scottish castle alone with a woman—especially one with a notorious mother.

Dougal was not too happy with the scheme. 'Are you sure about this, Poppy? It doesn't feel right leaving you alone.'

'I think Miss Ramsay is more than capable of looking after herself, or so she keeps telling me.'

Poppy lifted her chin. 'Yes, I am.' Allowing her frozen expression to melt into a warm smile, she turned to Dougal. 'I'll be fine, just don't forget I'm here.'

'If you say so... I had strict instructions to bring you back.'

Poppy pressed a kiss to his bearded cheek. 'Where am I going to go?'

Dougal enfolded her in a bearlike hug, swinging her off the ground. The uncomplicated warmth of the spontaneous gesture of affection brought a teary glaze to Poppy's eyes as she hugged him back.

Setting his teeth together, Gianluca endured the tender scene, a growl locked in his throat.

'Perhaps,' he suggested, 'we should make a move now. Then you can return for Miss Ramsay.'

Dougal cast a wistful look at the kettle, but agreed with the suggestion.

Gianluca followed the other man to the door and then turned back to Poppy. 'I'll sort the press—it might take some time but we'll meet up very soon, I promise, *cara*. What's your mobile number?'

Poppy reeled off the digits automatically, noticing he didn't jot them down.

'I assume that you'll be staying with your grandmother in the village?'

She nodded. 'I would think so, unless she wants to come straight back here.'

'Stall her.'

Oh, yes, and that was going to be so easy.

CHAPTER ELEVEN

Two hours later Poppy was sitting in the small boat as they chugged across the choppy seas of the sea loch towards the whitewashed village, the cat in a basket on her lap.

'When we got off the boat it was total chaos,' Dougal was telling her. 'They were swarming everywhere. I don't mind telling you I was fair scared out of my wits when those bulbs started flashing, but the man he didn't even blink! God, but he's a cool customer.'

He flashed Poppy a sideways glance and she dutifully agreed with his admiring assessment. 'Yes, he is.'

'And when they started sticking the microphones right in his face, mind the man—he just smiled.' Dougal gave a quiet chuckle.

'So are there a lot of people...press still there?'

'Don't you worry. One of his people came out as I was leaving and said he'd give a press conference up in the village hall.' He consulted his watch. 'About now, so there won't be a soul outside.'

'His people?'

'Aye, there were loads of them, some with the walkie-talkie ear-piece things, waiting when he arrived. I think they were expecting to be organising transport for a corpse.' He saw Poppy shiver and said hastily, 'Sorry, love, it must have been grim out there during the storm.'

To Poppy's relief the subject switched to the weather, a theme that lasted until they reached the village.

Fergus and his wife Emma owned the village store. They were both delighted to see her. Her grandmother's welcome offered less hugs and more stern lectures.

She pronounced herself sad she had produced a granddaughter with so little common sense and thought for others.

But it turned out a lot easier than she had anticipated to get her grandmother to stay over in the village. The reason became obvious when she got to her feet.

A slight sprain, nothing more, Isabel Ramsay had announced, revealing a heavily strapped ankle.

She could, she declared, after warning her grand-daughter not to fuss, get around fine with the aid of a stick, but the stairs at the castle might, she admitted, prove a problem and the castle did not boast a bathroom on the ground floor, otherwise she would have been quite comfortable sleeping on the sofa.

'Now, tell me, what about Gianluca—when did he turn up?'

'He's not dead.'

'Of course he's not dead! I didn't think for one sec-ond he was, though nobody would listen to me. I told Flora the same thing. I told her that boy always did have more lives than a cat. If he'd been going to kill him-self he'd have done it years ago, all those crazy stunts he used to get up to with you,' she said, directing a sly look at her granddaughter's face.

'And he's so good-looking. It's such a waste—he

should marry again. Flora thinks so too. What do you think?'

'I think, Gran, it's none of my business.'

Helping out behind the counter in the shop that afternoon, Poppy saw firsthand how much media interest the rumour of Luca's demise followed by his miraculous reappearance had created.

When he did not vanish as anticipated in one of the bullet-proof chauffeur-driven limousines that had appeared in the village, but stayed, taking up residence with his entourage in a local hotel, so did the journalists. The story seemed set to run and run—there wasn't a news bulletin that didn't have some reference to him.

She was closing up the shop that evening when the phone in her pocket began to vibrate. Pulling down the shutter on the door, she pulled it out and lifted it to her ear.

'Hello, *cara*.'

The familiar rich warm voice the other end drew a silent sigh from her lips. 'Luca,' she breathed shakily. 'You called…?'

There was a short static silence. 'Did I not say I would…?'

Poppy nodded, then remembered he couldn't see her. 'Yes, but you didn't write down my number and—'

'I have a very good memory.'

'So how are you…? I saw you on the telly this afternoon. I had no idea that you were so important in a you-get-a-cold-and-the-bottom-drops-out-of-the-market sort of way.'

His voice, deep and tinged with impatience, cut across her. 'I want to see you.'

Poppy swallowed. 'I want to see you too,' she admitted huskily.

'I had planned for you to join me here tonight, but the damned press are everywhere... I'll work something out, I promise. Are you all right?'

Poppy wanted to yell, No, I'm not bloody all right, you stupid man, I love you! 'I'm fine, Luca, and Gran...'

'I know. I spoke to her on the phone earlier. She is totally irrepressible, isn't she? She read me the Riot Act and predicted my early demise. The ankle is really not too bad, then?'

'She says not... You spoke to Gran?'

'She offered to call you, but I did not wish to speak to you while you were standing in a room full of people.'

Poppy gave a bitter laugh. 'Why not? This is hardly phone sex, is it?' She shook her head and grimaced into the receiver. 'Sorry,' she gritted through clenched teeth. The last thing she wanted to do was alienate him by being bitchy and naggy. 'I was just—'

'I am frustrated too.'

Poppy gave a sigh of relief. 'God, yes...' She stopped as the sound of voices in the background drifted down the line. 'Well, thank you,' Luca said in a totally different voice. 'I will speak to you very soon.'

After the initial press conference Gianluca did not reappear, and when his camp did not offer as much as a sound bite for the waiting press it might have been expected that they drift away. That had certainly been the strategy, and a few did, but to Luca's intense frustration the bulk remained.

His desperation to see Poppy made him take the risk

that he knew was unwise, but, the alternative being he go quietly mad, he did anyway.

Poppy was walking Flora along the beach road that next evening when he appeared, materialising out of nowhere. She gave a choked gasp, dropped the stick she had been about to throw for the dog and stared up at him, her heart climbing into her throat.

Dressed all in black, the light salty breeze blowing in from the loch ruffling his dark hair, he looked simultaneously sinister and sexy. Her heart performed another flip.

'Heel!' he said sternly to the dog that greeted him with rapturous enthusiasm.

Poppy's greeting was more restrained. She was so concerned about keeping her emotions in check and not making a total fool of herself—*again*—that she didn't register the tension in his lean body or the telling tautness in his jaw.

He had spoken to Gran again that morning on the phone. She'd been talking about the grants that he had apparently told her were available to repair historic monuments ever since, but he had not asked to speak to her.

'Should you be here?'

Gianluca scanned her face, hungrily eating up the details, not registering the frigid note of hurt in her voice. 'I had to be here. I needed…' She heard him mutter something that sounded like 'to hell with this' before he grabbed her.

'Now that,' he said, releasing her after delivering a deep, passionate, mind-numbing kiss, 'I probably shouldn't have done in public.'

Slightly mollified, she nodded. 'Probably not.'

'I've arranged tomorrow night for a car to pick you up—'

'No!'

He looked startled and so was she—until she opened her mouth Poppy hadn't known she was going to say it. Now she had she knew it was the right thing.

'You don't know what I'm going to say.'

She tipped her head in acknowledgement. 'But I do know it will be some furtive creep-around-through-the-back-door arrangement...' His expression said it all. 'Well, I'm not happy with that. It makes me feel... uncomfortable.'

He looked down at her in frustration. 'I'm doing this for you.'

She dismissed his words with a wave of her hand. 'I'm going back to London in the morning.'

'You can't!' The protest was dragged from somewhere deep inside him.

'Why not, Luca?' she asked him quietly. All she wanted was him to ask her to stay, not *assume* she would; that was all it would take.

There was a short silence. 'Because we are going to work out a strategy to save the castle—we agreed, Poppy.'

She shook her head and gave a small bitter laugh. 'You don't need me to do that.

'Your name can open doors that would never open for me. You look at red tape and it dissolves and we both know that you'll do whatever you have to—throw money at it, make a deal, bribe someone...whatever— and don't think I'm not grateful because you'll save Gran's home, but, please,' she begged throatily, 'don't insult me by pretending you need my help. Gran might be fooled by this talk of grants but I'm not. Just please don't let her find out that you're footing the bill.'

'It isn't that simple.'

'But you've already set the wheels in motion?'

He tipped his head in abrupt acknowledgement.

She expelled a gusty sigh and straightened her shoulders. 'So it's sorted,' she said, adopting a cheerful attitude. 'And Gran's happy to stay here, at least until her ankle is healed, but I'm in danger of outstaying my welcome. So this is really goodbye.'

Gianluca stared at the hand she extended towards him and shook his head. 'It's not goodbye, I...' He stopped as two men in suits began to run along the beach towards him.

Luca, his face like thunder, walked towards them.

Poppy watched as they spoke. Whatever they said it did not appear to please Luca, who after a few moments glanced over his shoulder in her direction before turning and walking briskly in the opposite direction without a backward glance.

His actions hurt like a slap in the face. At least it was a wake-up call... Did she really want to be the girl expected to fade into the background when her presence was deemed unnecessary?

He had reached the other end of the beach when the news crew his security had told him was responding to a tip-off caught up with him. To his relief Poppy had vanished.

About a million no comments later he arrived back at his hotel.

CHAPTER TWELVE

Poppy waved goodbye to Fergus and Emma, resisting a crazy impulse to duck down in her seat of her taxi as she drove past the hotel where Luca was staying. For all she knew he had probably already left—maybe that was what the calls she had not picked up last night had been about—and he was even now being whisked away, no doubt in a blacked-out car flanked by bodyguards.

It was a life but not as she knew it.

For about five minutes it had seemed as if they occupied the same planet, but the events of the past few days had made it abundantly clear that they did not.

She had done the right thing. She didn't want to be with a man who was too embarrassed to acknowledge she existed. It was just a pity that the right thing hurt so much.

Luca's decision to drive himself back to London had caused a minor furore among his anxious staff, who were showing inexplicable signs of mass anxiety and a sudden irritating desire to wrap him in cotton wool.

He had done what he had to and not what he wanted to for a couple of days. He had turned the charm on for the media and restored the share price by appearing live on television—something he never normally did. He had phoned his family—this involved a great deal of tears and almost as many remonstrations, which he had meekly accepted.

Now it was time to do what he wanted, and he wanted Poppy.

The news delivered by his godmother that she had already left was a minor setback.

The journey to the railway station that should have taken him half an hour took him double—the road was covered with roadworks and several sets of traffic lights, which all turned red as he approached.

Forced to sit, wait, he found it hard not to take the delays personally. By the time he reached his destination he had begun to realise how seemingly sane people were on occasion driven to buy into conspiracy theories!

Perhaps he was not meant to catch Poppy...?

Not a man inclined to meekly accept his fate, actually not a man who believed in fate or destiny, Gianluca glanced at his watch and looked around for a parking space. He was not just cutting it fine, he was... Then he saw a parking space and gave a grunt of satisfaction. He was due a bit of luck.

He released his seat belt and began to scan the crowds, his long fingers beating out an impatient tattoo on the steering wheel. There were too many people moving in and out of the terminal building to pick out one small one. He was reaching for the door handle when in the rear-view mirror a group of noisy teenage schoolboys moved to cross the road and she was there. As he watched she had stopped to transfer her large canvas bag from one hand to the other, tossing her head to shake her glossy ponytail back over her shoulder and losing her balance slightly, until some passing guy in a suit placed a hand on her waist.

It seemed to Gianluca that this stranger's hand stayed on the cinched waist of her red jacket far longer than was necessary and the smile of gratitude he received for his trouble was over the top.

The stranger paused and watched her, tugging at the collar of his shirt, as she moved on, but Poppy remained totally oblivious to the effect of her smile and the lecherous eyes directed towards her denim-covered rear. Her skinny designer jeans fitted rather too well, emphasising the curve of her bottom and the feminine flare of her hips.

Gianluca fought the crazy impulse to leap out and confront the stranger and he swore softly under his breath before he leaned across to open the passenger door. She was close enough now for him to hear the clicking sound of the heels of her ankle boots on the pavement.

The wheelie arrangement on her bag had jammed and, forced to carry it, Poppy was wishing she had not packed quite so many shoes. The lopsided posture she was forced to adopt was making the base of her spine ache.

Approaching the busy entrance to the station, she turned her head in response to the prolonged honking of a taxi horn in time to see the driver stick his head out of the window and deliver a vocal protest.

The protest was directed at the driver of the car who pulled his car into a space beside her reserved for taxis.

The car itself was some sleek low-slung metallic silver monster that would not have looked out of place on a racing circuit. It looked very out of place outside the provincial railway station.

The door of the car almost brushed her leg as it swung open.

'Get in!'

Poppy's heart lurched. The voice was more heavily accented than normal, it seemed to her, but still totally unmistakeable.

For the space of several heartbeats she stood frozen like a small statue until a gulping gasp left her lips and her nerveless fingers released their grip on the holdall.

The driver, dark, sleek and grim-faced, leaned across to repeat the terse command. Every synapse in her skull started firing off messages simultaneously as her brain tipped into wild panic.

'Get in, Poppy.' He sounded bored.

'Luca…? How…?' She took a deep breath and lifted her chin and met his eyes and rapidly changed her mind about the bored. The anger smouldering in the dark depths was hard to miss—not that she could see what he had to be angry about…

'I don't think so.'

Her brain was emerging from total shutdown but her heart continued to beat so fast in reaction to the shock of seeing him that it felt as if she had a wild bird trapped in her chest.

'I am not asking you to think.'

Just as well.

'I am asking you to get in the car.'

Poppy gave a bitter little laugh. Asking? He was telling—*so no change there!* 'As you ask so charmingly— no.' She bared her teeth in a cold smile.

He swore under his breath, and Poppy shook her head in mock disapproval. 'Someone got out of bed the wrong side this morning.'

'The wrong bed,' he corrected under his breath, then added louder, 'I got out of the wrong bed.' Not strictly accurate. Actually he had not got out of any bed—he had not slept. 'It should have been your bed.'

A tiny gasp left her lips. 'What makes you think you can talk to me like that?' The answer was the excitement squirming in her belly.

He could deal with the animosity in her glare because it was mingled with an equal measure of longing. 'Because it's what you want too—you want me in your bed.'

The arrogance of his retort sent the mortified colour rushing to her cheeks. 'Could you say that any louder? I think that a man getting on the Crewe train didn't hear you and the lady with the hearing aid might have missed the last bit.'

'I'm amazed you want to risk being seen with me in a public place.' He was already drawing a lot of attention, but if anyone realised who was driving the monster car the attention would zoom off the scale.

The furrow above his hawkish nose deepened. 'What are you talking about?'

'A Ranieri and the daughter of a notorious mother?'

'What has your mother got to do with this? You don't still think I slept with her?'

The reminder of the earlier suspicion made her flush. 'No, I don't. Now, please, go away!' she hissed, casting a furtive look over her shoulder. 'People are staring! And what do you expect when you drive some stupid car that probably cost a hundred thousand pounds?'

The abrupt change of subject made him blink. 'Rather more than that, actually.'

Poppy, speaking across him, continued her denunciation. 'Goes a billion miles an hour and looks like a spaceship.'

'You do not like my car?' He sounded amused rather than offended by the possibility.

Any second now someone was going to realise who he was and people would start recording the moment on their mobile phones. Her stomach muscles tightened in sick anticipation of this moment. 'I don't like being stared at.'

Welcome to my world, he thought. 'They will stare a lot more when I pick you up and throw you in.' The accompanying image of this action that formed in his head sent a strong pulse of lust through his body. 'And yes...' He paused, flashed her a white wolfish grin that made her stomach flip, before adding softly, 'I would.'

Poppy met the dark shadowed eyes, almost tempted to call his bluff.

'I don't respond well to threats!' she told him haughtily.

'It was intended to be more in the nature of a promise.'

Watching her staring at him, her big eyes reminding him of a trapped fawn, Gianluca was filled with a strong desire to follow through with his threat, to feel her soft body in his arms, hear her heartbeat, enjoy the warm passion of her response to him.

'What do you think I'm going to do, Poppy? This is a public place...' Possibly, given the thoughts going through his head, a good thing.

He produced what Poppy supposed was his version

of a harmless puppy smile, only in his case the puppy would grow up to be a big bad wolf—he already had.

'Fine.' She consulted her watch and added frigidly, 'Two minutes.'

His nostrils flared at the stipulation but he made no comment, not even when the bag she lobbed into the car glanced off his shoulder.

I hope it hurt, she thought viciously as she ducked her head and slid into the passenger seat, sinking immediately into the deep leather upholstery of the bucket seat. Crossing one booted foot over the other, she directed a cold look at his profile.

'I think he wants this parking space,' she said, indicating the taxi driver who was flashing his lights. 'Look, what did you want to say?' She glanced at her watch. 'Because your two minutes is almost up.'

He nodded in the direction of the gesticulating taxi driver, gave a Latin gesture of his own in response, then proceeded to crunch the gears.

There was a short time delay before the relevance of the noise hit Poppy. She broke off, her eyes widening just as he began to reverse rapidly out of the space.

'Stop this car immediately!' she yelled, banging her hand on the state-of-the-art dashboard to emphasise her point.

Gianluca glanced her way, holding her eyes for a brief moment before planting his foot on the accelerator. The car shot forward into the traffic flow.

'Fasten your seat belt, Poppy.'

His voice sounded calm. The gleam she had seen in his heavy-lidded eyes had not been calm, it had been... A shudder snaked its way up her spine. Poppy lifted a hand to her throat where a blue veined pulse was throbbing. She was shaking.

There was zero chance that he hadn't noticed.

'I'm not going to fasten my seat belt. My train leaves in ten minutes!' she wailed, agitation causing her to literally bounce in the deeply upholstered leather seat.

'I have to tell you that, while it might be a fascinating subject, railway timetabling holds little interest for me,' Gianluca drawled at his driest.

Poppy's laugh had an edge of hysteria. 'So sorry to bore you.' Like a trapped animal, she let her glance slide to the door handle.

'Don't bother, it's locked.'

She turned her head jerkily towards him; Gianluca was looking straight ahead. 'I'm not insane...' *Maybe I am—I got in the car.* 'I'm not about to jump out of a moving car.'

His heavy-lidded eyes met hers in the driving mirror. The bottom fell out of Poppy's stomach, leaving a black, squooshy, empty space where it had been.

'This is silly, Gianluca. What are you doing?' she asked, struggling to channel calm.

There was no need to panic—after all, what was the worst that could happen?

The answer to her silent question made her groan— he could touch her and she could melt, dissolve like a bowl of ice cream in the sun and scream, Why don't you love me?

'I am trying to concentrate.' Gianluca wrenched his wandering eyes from the curve of her denim-covered thigh and trained it grimly on the road ahead where several streams of heavy traffic were merging, the frustrated drivers all reluctant to give way.

He had stopped short of saying, So shut up—just—but it was implicit in his abrupt response.

Poppy clenched her teeth and flung him a look of loathing. 'Wait until I start singing.'

The bizarre threat caused the grim lines bracketing his mouth to relax fractionally. 'I have rarely felt so intimidated.'

'You mock, now, but you won't be laughing for long...' Poppy trained her eyes on her hands folded in her lap as her thoughts drifted back to those long-off schooldays. 'I was in the school choir.' Back row because the front row was for the pretty girls. 'But only to make up the numbers. I had strict instructions to mime.'

Laughter came easier now than it had back then, but one of the first lessons a plumpish schoolgirl learnt was it was easier to laugh at yourself before someone else had the chance to.

Momentarily distracted, Gianluca allowed his eyes to brush her glossy bowed head. 'Harsh.'

'Not really. I had...have a terrible singing voice. We are talking once heard never forgotten. I'm just not musical.'

A buried memory from the past surfaced in his head: a heather-clad hillside, the kid with bare feet, her arms lifted above her head, swirling wildly to the beat of a pop tune being played on the small old-fashioned cassette player propped up on a rocky outcrop.

'That's not true—you can dance.'

Her startled gaze flew to his face. 'How would you know...? I mean, I can't as such. I *like* to dance but I've never actually learnt...just a few salsa classes.'

The work colleague who had persuaded her to go along had dropped out after that first lesson, miffed because she'd thought Poppy had been holding out—there was no way, she'd insisted, that Poppy was a beginner *and* she had totally monopolised the handsome dance teacher.

It had, she had claimed, been embarrassing.

Despite the jibe, Poppy had gone back the next week alone.

'You can tell by the way someone moves that they can dance.' There was a graceful fluidity to the way Poppy moved.

Poppy responded to this suggestion with a derisive snort. 'And I suppose you can tell by the way I talk I can't sing.'

The muscles along his strong jaw tightened as he trained his eyes on the road ahead. 'You have a…pleasant voice.' Men immune to her throaty laugh or husky stammer would be difficult to find.

'Well, I don't have a *pleasant* singing voice… The music sounds great in my head. The problem starts when I open my mouth, and this is an enclosed space.'

'Look, if you want to sing, fine…sing along with Puccini.' He pressed a button and the mellifluous voice of a famous tenor filled the car. 'And I couldn't stop the car here even if I wanted to.' He nodded outside where men with drills and dumper trucks lined the narrow single lane of traffic. 'So just relax and enjoy the music.'

Relax!

The sound of Poppy's laugh was drowned out by the romantic aria. She blamed the sudden sting of tears she blinked back on the romantic crescendo of suffering— it always made her cry.

CHAPTER THIRTEEN

Normal flow of traffic resumed on the outskirts of the town. Gianluca expected Poppy to renew her objections but she remained silent beside him. The reason for this uncharacteristic reticence was revealed when he flashed a glance her way.

Head a little to one side, her eyes were closed, her dark lashes fanned out across the curve of her smooth cheeks.

Lowering the volume of the music to a background hum, he turned off the main road and onto a lane that skirted a loch. He drove on a few miles before drawing onto a gravelled parking area beside a scenic viewing point.

It was deserted apart from a motorbike. The young couple it belonged to were standing at the viewing point taking photos of the dramatic mountain panorama. He could hear their shared laughter.

Gianluca studied Poppy's sleeping profile for a moment before switching off the engine. Sleep made her look incredibly vulnerable.

She stirred but did not immediately wake, and he did not wake her, but continued to watch her, the soft regular rise and fall of her breasts, the fluttering of her dark lashes against her lightly flushed cheeks.

A strand of hair had fallen across her face. Drifting near her lips, it stirred when she breathed. He reached out and pushed it away, his fingertips grazing the downy softness of her cheek.

She opened her eyes and blinked in sleepy confusion.

'Nice nap?'

Poppy's eyes connected with a pair of dark eyes.

Suddenly wide awake, she stiffened and shot bolt upright in her seat.

'What...how...?' She looked beyond Gianluca, registering the mountain vista. 'I wasn't asleep, I was just—'

'Resting your eyes?'

The sardonic suggestion drew a scowl. Scrubbing the eyes in question with her fist, she stifled a yawn. 'I didn't sleep much last night.'

An expression her sleepy brain struggled to interpret moved across Gianluca's lean face. 'Neither, as a matter of fact, did I. Would you like to look at the view?'

Poppy exhaled a long shaky breath and turned her head fixing him with a narrow-eyed glittering stare. 'If I were you I'd avoid being near any steep drops with me.'

He raised his brows. 'You are annoyed with me?'

'Are you totally mad, Luca?'

His lips quivered into a smile that held more than a hint of self-mockery as he considered his actions. 'It is, I think, a possibility.' Some might say probability. 'I wanted to talk to you.'

'So you kidnapped me...sure, that makes sense,' she

drawled. 'If you're some egotistical power-mad lunatic who thinks normal rules don't apply to him.'

During this breathless speech Gianluca's eyes had slid from her face to the large daisy emblazoned across the chest of her black tee shirt. The daisy was moving in time with her agitated breathing. His eyes lifted to her mouth. Her full parted lips were coloured appropriately poppy red; the colour was echoed in the length of velvet ribbon that confined her hair on the crown of her head.

Poppy folded her arms across her chest, biting back a wince as the actions squashed her shamelessly engorged nipples. 'So what was so important that you deemed it necessary to kidnap me?'

'I want to talk and as you show a marked inclination to run away...'

She crossed one booted ankle over the other. 'So you wanted to talk...go ahead?'

'Why didn't you answer my calls, Poppy?'

Her eyes flickered sideways. 'There was nothing to say.'

'We agreed—'

With an angry little gasp she twisted in her seat, remembering the crushing sense of rejection she had felt when he walked away from her without an explanation. 'There is no *we*. You don't walk away from someone without a word when there is a *we*!' she yelled.

'That!' His face cleared. 'I had to walk away—someone tipped off a news crew that I was on the beach. Can you imagine what it would have been like if you had been there? I wanted to protect you from that.'

'Protect your family name, you mean!'

He shook his head in confusion. 'You have lost me.'

'My mum is notorious and your family is—'

'Bloody irrelevant as far as I'm concerned.'

Poppy blinked at the force behind his pronounce-
ment. 'I don't give a damn who your mother is or your
father or the colour of your damned cat. We had great
sex. I wanted more—I wanted you, but I didn't want to
expose you to the sort of media scrutiny women I sleep
with attract. It would make your email debacle look like
a walk in the park.'

'Oh...'

He gave a pleased smile. 'Exactly. *Oh.*'

Poppy did not immediately register that he had
turned the ignition. Her thoughts were elsewhere as
she struggled to get her head around the facts he had
given her, struggling to think at all when her brain was
clouded by a constant fog of sexual awareness... Any
future discussion with Luca should not be made in an
enclosed space.

Future—was there a future?

She shook her head. 'No!'

Luca turned his head. 'No what?'

Belatedly she became aware of the softly purring
engine. 'Where are you taking me?'

'I have a lodge outside Stirling.'

Poppy shook her head. 'I'm not going anywhere with
you, Luca.' The indecision gone, she suddenly felt extremely calm.

The note of finality in her soft voice brought a wary
furrow to Luca's brow; with a sigh he switched off the
engine. 'So what now?'

'I don't want to be your one-night stand.'

'Neither do I.'

'So what do you want me to be?'

'We can continue to—'

Poppy shook her head firmly and held up her hands in a defensive gesture as he leaned in towards her. 'You want a mistress, Luca... Do you even want to be exclusive?'

'You leave me no energy for other women, *cara.*'

Her laugh was painful for him to hear.

'A good answer, but not to my question. Have you actually thought this thing through, Luca? Am I to have other lovers too?'

'No!'

She lifted her brows at his outraged response and added quietly, 'I wouldn't want any. I wouldn't want any man but you, Luca, because the fact is I have always loved you. Yes, I know I'm not meant to say that.'

Luca sat beside her, his chin on his chest, not moving, not saying a word. Unable to read his opaque mask, she took a deep breath and plunged on.

'But I want to be with you so much that I thought I could do it on your terms, but I know now I was wrong. I want more...much more... I want a man who is prepared to be open to the possibility of love. I want the *possibility* of marriage and children.

'The big question is what do you want, Luca? What are you prepared to give? What are you prepared to sacrifice?'

Luca continued to stare at his hands as he had done the entire time she had been speaking.

'I need time.'

It was more, much more, than she had expected. 'Take your time, but remember, I'm not sure how long

I'm prepared to wait… I've already waited most of my life.'

She took a deep shuddering breath and felt a mixture of exhilaration and fear. She had taken a gamble and only time would tell if it would pay off.

Without a word he pressed the ignition.

'The station?'

'Please.' She was a well-brought-up girl; her manners were beautiful even when her heart was breaking…no, not breaking, just cracked and severely bruised… All he needed was time.

The return journey to the station was made in total silence.

As he pulled into a parking space, legitimately this time, he turned his head her way. 'Poppy…?' He stopped and shook his head as though he had changed his mind about whatever he had been going to say.

It was only when she unbuckled her seat belt that he leaned towards her, his eyes not leaving hers as he reached out and pulled the red ribbon from her hair. His eyes left hers then to follow the movement of her hair as it tumbled around her shoulders.

He gave a sigh of pleasure low in his throat and slid one hand into her hair, tangling his fingers into the silky tendrils.

Poppy, unable to move, unable to blink, stared into his dark eyes and felt dizzy, her throat ached, every muscle in her body tensed in anticipation of what was coming next—it had to come next or she might die of sheer wanting. Her racing heart climbed into her aching throat as his free hand slid down the curve of her back.

When he bent his head and moved his lips softly over

the surface of her mouth she whimpered and clutched at his front. He pulled back and looked directly into her eyes. Whatever he saw there caused his own eyes to darken. A low growl vibrated in his throat as he reclaimed her lips. This time the kiss was not soft, but hard and demanding, his tongue sinking deep between her lips, probing the warm recesses of her mouth.

They broke apart and sat there, both breathing hard as though they had just sprinted for the finishing line.

Poppy pushed the door open, warning huskily, 'I'm not sure how long I can wait, Luca.'

CHAPTER FOURTEEN

POPPY smiled through the volley of flashes as previously instructed and held onto the dramatic sweeping skirt of her scarlet dress that blended seamlessly into the carpet her spiky heels sank into.

'Is it always this mad?' she whispered to the man beside her through her fixed smile.

He flashed a smile over the top of her glossy head. 'I don't know—I usually avoid these things like the plague.'

Poppy stopped dead in the middle of the red carpet, one of the artful tendrils left out of the simple twist secured with several hundred hairgrips on top of her head wafting across her face as she directed a startled stare up at her escort, who looked handsome and distinguished in his dinner jacket, his silver hair coaxed into a semblance of order for the occasion.

'But George said that you—' She blew at the determined tendril as it tickled her nose.

'George said, did he? And what did my dear son say?' Charles Semple caught Poppy's elbow, murmuring, 'If we stop I think it's possible we get trampled over. They just keep coming—'

'George said—'

'No, don't tell me, let me guess—George said please go with Dad because he'll look like a sad loser walking down the red carpet alone when his ex is going to be there with her new younger-model lover.'

'Pretty much,' Poppy admitted. 'He also said you lived for these occasions.'

'Dear George,' his fond parent murmured. 'He said you were heartbroken and in danger of becoming a recluse and also sinking into deep depression if your friends didn't show you that there was life outside your flat.'

'I'll kill him!' Poppy exclaimed, thinking that in her case George had pretty much got it right, though, as far as she was concerned, recluses got a bad press.

There were major pluses to working from home. Since word got out she was available she was snowed under—she had refused Phil's offer, though, partly because two weeks after she had returned home Poppy had discovered why her boobs were feeling so sore and the smell of coffee made her rush for the bathroom.

Nobody knew her news, though she had been tempted to tell her half-brother, holding back only because she had this crazy idea that the father should be the first to know.

Of Luca there had been no word.

It looked very much as if her gamble had not paid off and Poppy was wishing she had remembered sooner the old adage don't gamble what you're not prepared to lose.

It really did look as if she had lost...but she still had his baby. It was the knowledge of the life growing inside her that had kept her going during the past few weeks.

If he didn't contact her soon she knew she was going

to have to make the first move, the man needed to know he was going to be a father.

'In a slow and painful fashion,' George's loving parent agreed. 'The hell of it is he means well.'

'I know.' Poppy's fixed fake smile melded into a genuine grin as she met the eyes of her half-brother's dad and laughed.

It was the shot that appeared on the pages of numerous newspapers the next day with captions that identified the beautiful girl with the famous director as his infamous first wife's daughter.

It was the image that Gianluca saw as he stepped onto the red carpet.

A wave of white-hot rage washed over him so intense and consuming that he found himself inside the building without having any memory of how he had got there.

The film being premiered was being spoken of as a contender for Oscars. At the end of the screening he didn't have a clue what it was about but he did know how many times the man with Poppy had bent his head and whispered something in her ear, how many times he had touched her shoulder or arm. He also knew how many times she had smiled at something he said and how many times her soft husky laughter had drawn curious eyes.

She was clearly having a great time, while he had been going through hell and she had been hooking up with some guy who was quite frankly old... The age gap was to his mind obscene.

And the irony was presumably he had facilitated this. He had slept with her and awoken a dormant sensuality she was now sharing with, for all he knew, half the male population of the City. The hell of it was she looked happy and relaxed with the old guy.

As the credits rolled at his side his starry-eyed niece gave a sigh.

'That was incredible! So sad and James Litton is so hot. Thank you for bringing me, Uncle Gianluca.'

'I'm glad you enjoyed...' he responded mechanically while still staring three rows ahead where Poppy, her shoulders smooth and bare above a sexy red number that appeared to have been painted on her body, sat. 'That man over there, Dina—do you know who he is?'

'Which one?'

'The one with the silver hair sitting in the—'

'That's Charlie Semple,' she said immediately.

'And who,' Gianluca said, struggling for patience and wondering how in a moment of weakness he had succumbed to the blatant moral blackmail of his sister and brought Dina here as a birthday treat, 'is Charlie Semple?'

'You're kidding? You don't know who—'

'Clearly I do not.'

'He's a film director.'

Gianluca shook his head.

'God, you're clueless.' The teenager seemed amused by his ignorance, and eager to display her superior knowledge. 'He's got *three* Oscars and everyone said he should for certain have had one last year for *My Beloved.*' She went on to list the other films he directed, displaying an encyclopaedic knowledge of the subject that made Gianluca wonder when she actually did any work at the expensive school his sister and her banker husband had chosen to send her when they had settled in London the previous summer. Dina had not lost her American accent.

Gianluca tuned out her youthful chatter. He had previously thought teenage girls sulked—this one talked, incessantly. He knew all he needed—the only question was what was he going to do about it?

He was hindered in his plans by the necessity of delivering his chatty niece safely home first.

When Charlie suggested they put in an appearance at a famous jazz club where the after-premiere party was being held Poppy at first said she'd pass.

His 'Why not?' made her think, *Why not?* Life went on, Gianluca clearly had gone wherever and with whoever... She didn't care—it was about time she got out there and one of the most glamorous parties on the social calendar was as good a time as any.

'It's a shame to waste the dress.' She glanced down. She had spotted the vintage fifties dress in a window twelve months earlier and had walked in and bought it—this was the first, which made one more than she had expected, opportunity she had had to wear it. Who knew? It might never fit her post-baby figure. Hard to think post baby when her waistline was still slim and her belly flat.

'Excellent, and we can use the occasion to plan our revenge on George.'

Despite her initial nervousness about what a big glitzy showbiz party would be like—actually a lot of fun—she surprised herself by enjoying it in a star-struck way.

It helped that Charlie, who was a lot more famous than she had ever realised, was undemanding company, and as the evening progressed Poppy found herself feeling more relaxed than she had in weeks—right up to the moment when he walked in.

She *felt* his presence in a tingly-sensation-down-her-back sort of way that was hard to describe several seconds before she actually caught sight of him. Even with the warning nothing could have prepared her for the numbing shock that coursed through her body when she turned her head and saw him standing there.

There were any number of handsome men attending the party tonight but to her, admittedly less than objective, mind Luca made every other man in the room fade into insignificance. As she watched he flicked his cuff to reveal the face of his watch and frowned. He looked up, his dark smouldering glance connecting with her own, and Poppy stopped breathing as a jolt of lustful longing stabbed hard directly through her defenceless heart.

In his formal dinner jacket, his white shirt affording a dramatic contrast to his bronzed skin, he looked supremely elegant, sleek, expensive and jaw-droppingly gorgeous and also totally furious.

She stood there, her paralysed nervous system not up to functioning beyond the basic breathe-do-not-fall-down mode as he walked straight across to her, not looking to right or left and blanking the several people who greeted him, the entire time his black stare trained like a heat-seeking missile directly on her face.

'This is a surprise,' she said brightly as he approached.

All the things he had planned on saying went out of his head the moment he heard her voice. Instead of the dignified but blighting comment he had intended to make he heard himself growl.

'*Dio*, the man is old enough to be your father. What the hell do you think you're doing?'

Poppy blinked and thought, *So not in the mood for small talk.*

'If it was any of your business, which it isn't—' Poppy paused; the sound that emerged from his brown throat sounded suspiciously like a growl. 'Will you stop looking at me like that?' she said urgently. 'People are staring.'

He raised a sardonic brow. 'And you wore that dress because you wanted to fade into the background, I suppose.'

Two circles of bright angry colour appeared on her cheeks as she lifted her chin. Of all the nerve! Half the women here were wearing less than her—a lot less; she looked like a nun compared with some here!

'Sorry you don't like it,' she said, producing a smile of brilliant insincerity.

His heavy lids covered the glitter in his dark eyes as his glance slid down her body. 'I do like it and so does every other man in the room,' he contended throatily.

By the time his eyes had returned to her face the pink in Poppy's cheeks had spread to the heaving contours of the creamy slopes of her heaving bosom.

'I was actually enjoying myself until you arrived.'

'I know. I saw you *enjoying* yourself during the film and so did everyone else. You were making a total spectacle of yourself!' he charged.

'You were there!' Her eyes narrowed.

'Yes.'

'Alone?'

'No, not alone, I was with Dina.'

Poppy sucked in an angry breath. 'Well, and why

not? Off with the old, on with the new—unless Dina is special?'

'You're jealous!' The discovery curved his sensual lips into a smile of smug male satisfaction.

Poppy gave a tinkling laugh. 'This from the man who walked in here trailing his knuckles on the floor. I have to tell you the Neanderthal thing does not work for me,' she said, sounding bored.

'A problem, Poppy?' Charlie, smiling and urbane, appeared at her side, glass of champagne in his hand.

She took a deep breath and turned to him. 'No, everything's fine,' she lied, managing a shaky smile.

Charlie looked unconvinced. 'Want to dance?'

'No, she doesn't. We were talking.'

Gianluca's voice could have refrigerated volcanic lava.

Poppy had always liked George's dad, but her admiration increased tenfold as she watched him refuse to flinch. It was quite an achievement: if looks could kill he would be stretched out lifeless at Gianluca's feet.

'Are you going to introduce me to your friend, Poppy?'

Poppy squeezed Charlie's arm. 'He was actually just going.'

Gianluca looked from the fingers curved over the other man's arm to the message she was sending him with her eyes. The intimacy of the moment hit him; in a split second he saw that she was worried, not for herself, but for this guy... He had blown it.

The knowledge hit him with a force roughly equivalent to running full pelt into a solid wall.

'Yes,' he said abruptly. 'I was.'

* * *

Charlie offered to walk her up to her flat but Poppy declined. She waved goodbye to the departing taxi and approached the building where she lived, a sixties redbrick block.

Rather than wait for the lift, she took the stairs to her third-floor flat. Holding her skirt so that it didn't trail in the dust, she didn't immediately see the figure sitting with his back propped against her door, his head rested on his knees.

'Gianluca.' Her treacherous heart leapt at the sight of him.

His head lifted. 'You're home early and alone?'

'We all need a break from the relentless sex and debauchery once in a while,' she drawled sarcastically.

'I suppose I deserve that.'

She arched a brow. The explosive anger had gone and it was replaced by something she couldn't quite work out. 'You think?'

Gianluca dragged a hand through his hair, scrubbing it back and forth across his head. The dishevelled condition of the short dark hair standing in spikes suggested this was not the first time he'd done it.

Back pressed against the door, he pulled himself upright.

'Do you love him?'

Poppy stared. She had the impression that Gianluca was almost as surprised as she was by the question.

'The film-director guy—are you in love with him?'

'No.'

He closed his eyes, exhaled and nodded, then said rather obscurely, 'That's something,' before adding, 'Can I come in?'

She shook her head, ashamed because she wanted to

say yes, wanted to say it so much it hurt. 'I think you should go back to Dina or whoever…'

'Dina has to be up—she has school tomorrow.' He saw the shocked horror flash in her eyes and added drily, 'She's my niece, Poppy, and she wants to be an actress. Her parents are hoping she'll change her mind and settle for being a world-famous surgeon.'

'You went to the premiere with your niece.'

A wry smile touched his lips. 'I know, not really my style but my sister tricked me into it. My PA forgot the girl's last birthday and I am still paying.'

'Your *PA* forgot?'

The irony in her voice sailed over Gianluca's head. 'The women in my family are very manipulative.'

'If the men are anything like you they have to be. Why are you here, Luca, acting like…?'

'Acting like a complete fool?' he suggested.

Poppy gave a shaky laugh. 'Now that you mention it…yes.'

He levered himself off the wall and approached her, his hands extended but not trying to touch her. 'Have I completely blown it?' His jaw clenched as he waited for the answer his future depended on… What would he do if she said yes? She *couldn't* say yes.

Luca was asking *her* for *reassurance.* Luca humble—now that was weird on more levels than she could count. 'Blown what?'

She wasn't making this easy, but who could blame her? 'Us.'

The intensity of his scrutiny burned into her.

'You're asking me?' She framed her reply cautiously, still not sure if the rug was going to be pulled out from under her feet at any moment. Still not allowing herself to believe this was what she hoped. 'I thought I left that ball in your court.'

'Look, I know you've probably moved on with this Charlie Semple and—'

Poppy took a deep breath and decided to get that one out of the way. 'Charlie is George's dad.'

Luca's response was not one of relief. 'George!' he roared, forgetting his intention to be understanding and tolerant and if necessary beg.

He held onto the option of throttling both of these other guys in reserve.

'How many are there?' It had only been six weeks!

'George as in my half-brother George.'

A thunderstruck expression crossed Gianluca's face. He bit out a curse. 'So that guy…he…you weren't on a date?' He dragged a hand down his jaw and groaned.

Poppy pulled a bunch of keys out of her tiny bag and threw them at him. 'No, not a date.'

Gianluca automatically caught them one-handed. He looked from the keys in his hand to Poppy and angled a questioning brow.

'Open the door—my hands are shaking too much.' She held them out to show how much.

Gianluca looked at the white hands and he turned abruptly, his own hands not rock steady as he inserted the keys, opened the door and stood to one side to let her pass.

'What are you waiting for—an invitation?' she asked when he didn't follow. 'That would be a first.'

'Yes.' It was, as far as he was concerned, a night for firsts.

'Please come in, Luca.' *And stay, stay for ever.*

He stepped through the door that opened directly into the open-plan living area.

'Don't bother saying this is nice,' she said, making her voice hard—inside everything was shaking like jelly. 'Because I'm sure you didn't spend the last...how long were you sitting there anyhow?'

'Two hours.'

'Two hours on my doorstep because you want to discuss my décor.' The two hours in question had taken their toll. He still wore the same suit but it was now creased and dusty, his snowy shirt was open at the neck and his crumpled tie hung loose.

'I sat there because I want you and I would have spent a lot more than two hours to achieve this, though I think your suspicious neighbour across the corridor might by that point have called the police.'

'Mr Nasir, and we're all a bit cautious. There have been a lot of break-ins in the building.'

'I am not surprised about the break-ins. The lock—' he nodded towards the door '—is useless. I am not a career criminal and I could have got in—' He stopped and added, 'Obviously I didn't.'

'It didn't even cross your mind?' she teased.

He shrugged. 'All right, it crossed my mind.' At that moment so were other things and they were a lot more difficult to resist than house-breaking. 'You look incredible tonight.'

He wants me. The boned bodice of her dress suddenly felt extremely tight. She met his gaze.

His smile had a raw primitive quality that made her tummy muscles violently quiver as he continued to stare into her eyes. 'I wasn't sure if you'd wait, *cara*...?' He dragged a hand through his hair and thought, *So far not bad, Luca, but you could up your game, use the L word.*

Was he the only man in the world who found saying 'I love you' more terrifying than having a parachute fail at twenty thousand feet? At least with a parachute there was a back-up.

Her eyes shone. 'I have.' The time-limit thing had been a bluff. Poppy was pretty sure that she'd have waited all her life for Luca. 'I think you're my soul mate.' She half thought he might laugh, but he didn't.

'I think so too. I always wanted you. I wanted you when I married Aurelia. I never stopped...and she knew...I know she knew...'

The guilt and self-recrimination in his voice cut her like a blade.

'I was so stupid.' He shook his head as he considered the life choice he had made at twenty-three. 'I thought I was doing the *right* thing.

'You have no idea how many times I thought of you and what I had lost...then when I had the chance to have it again I very nearly...'

Poppy took his hand and laid it against the curve of her damp cheek.

'How am I doing here with the soul-bearing...?'

'Impressive,' she said, looking up at him through misted eyes.

'The family-duty thing—I fell for it totally. It was a total set-up,' he admitted. 'My dad made some bad... very bad business decisions. Without Aurelia's father's help he would have lost everything, gone to jail. If I married Aurelia that all went away.'

Poppy gasped in horror at the cold-blooded mercenary arrangement as she clutched Luca's hand between her own. 'Did Aurelia know about it?'

'Honest answer—I've no idea. If she did she never said.'

'It sounds as if she was a very troubled woman, Luca,' Poppy said quietly. 'But if she cared for you I'm sure she'd want you to be happy.'

'I know it's been weeks but I've been...I've been a gutless wonder.'

The frank admission drew a weak smile from Poppy.

'I sacrificed you...us, and then all it caused was misery.' He fixed her with a look that made her heart leap in her chest. 'I want you to know that when I tell you that I want to be a couple...exclusive couple...I want... to make you happy, Poppy, but hell my track record is not good!'

'Stop!' she pleaded, reaching up to take his face between her hands. 'This isn't about the past, it's about the future—our future... I love you very much.'

'And I love you, *cara mia*,' he husked, brushing her forehead with his lips before he lowered them to her mouth and kissed her deeply, with a passion and tenderness that shook her to the core.

When he released her she smiled and said, 'I always knew you did,' with such smug satisfaction that he laughed.

The laughter eased some of the tension in the room.

His voice was thick with emotion as he said, 'If I hurt you...I couldn't live with it.' There was a bleak finality to his words. 'When I think what we could have had... and I threw it all away.'

'We still could have it, Luca.' She took his big hand and gently laid it on her stomach.

He froze, his eyes slowly filling with shock as the significance of her action hit him, then incredulity as it sank in. '*Dio*, is it possible?' he asked in a raw voice of wonder.

She nodded.

He stared at her, paralysed, it seemed, by the information. 'A baby?'

'Our baby...'

'But how...? I was careful I...'

Poppy framed his face with her hands. 'The night when I came down to the kitchen...'

His eyes squeezed closed and he ejaculated rawly, 'I am not likely to forget.' He dampened his own jubilation and directed a cautious look at her face. 'And how do you feel about it? Are you well? Have you seen a doctor?'

'Great, yes, and yes in that order. I'm fine, Luca...a bit queasy but happy.'

'Truly?'

'When I thought you were not coming for me it was all that kept me going.'

He kissed her then, a kiss so tender that it brought tears to her eyes. 'I have missed you,' he said, trailing a finger down her smooth cheek.

'So why didn't you come for me sooner?'

His eyes slid from hers. 'There were reasons.'

Poppy shook her head, not willing to take his evasive answer. 'What reasons?'

He regarded her with ill-concealed frustration tinged with what she would have called embarrassment had it been anyone but Gianluca.

'Will you not take my word that until Monday I was unable to travel? I planned to see you tonight, then my sister hijacked me and played the you-forgot-your-only-niece's-birthday guilt card. I didn't even know I had an invite to the damned thing.'

Poppy refused to be distracted by the extra detail. 'No.'

His jaw tightened at the monosyllabic response.

'Fine,' he said, throwing up his hands in a gesture of defeat. 'I had...I was contagious.'

'How contagious?'

'I had chicken pox!'

Poppy stared. 'You had chicken pox?'

'Laugh, I can take it—my family thought it hilarious,' he revealed bitterly. 'It so happens that when contracted by an adult this childhood disease is anything but a laughing matter.' To be confined to his bed by a trivial childhood illness at such a moment had been one of the most frustrating and humiliating things in his entire life. 'You are laughing...?' he accused.

Poppy shook her head. 'No,' she promised, biting her lip. 'Well, only on the inside just a little,' she admitted, holding her forefinger and thumb a little apart to show him how little. 'You have to admit it's not a very... macho illness and you are very...' She let out a yelp as Gianluca, a growl vibrating in his throat, grabbed her and dragged her into his arms.

Her soft curves moulded themselves to the hard, lean lines of his body as she melted with a sigh into him. One hand on the back of her head, he looked down into her face.

'I am *very*?' he prompted throatily.

The lights dancing in his dark eyes made her head spin. 'You're...' With a moan she grabbed his face between her hands and pressed her mouth to his. 'You're beautiful,' she whispered against his mouth.

Unable to resist any longer, he slid his tongue between her parted lips, tasting her sweetness, deepening the pressure as the excitement built.

When they finally broke apart they were both breathing hard. 'I need to do that on a regular basis.'

His hand moved on a restless caressing sweep up and down the outer curve of her silk-clad thighs creating a friction that sent tingles through her entire body. 'What you said to me that day was quite the wake-up call.'

He suddenly let her go and walked across the room.

'I need to say things and I can't think when I'm touching you.'

The explanation made her feel better but not much. 'Fine,' she said, arranging her skirt as she sat down on the sofa.

'When you said you love me…I…that's the one thing I thought I never wanted to hear again. I caused the death of the last person who said that to me. I killed her—I killed my wife.' He saw the expression on Poppy's face and added, 'I know, not literally, but I didn't…love her. I married her knowing that, hoping it might happen…' He flashed her a look that made Poppy's tender heart bleed. 'But it couldn't because you already had my heart.

'Then she lost the baby and when she needed me I wasn't there, I was never there—she died from neglect.' He recounted this sequence of tragic events in an unemotional monotone that made Poppy yearn to hug him. When she thought of him carrying around this guilt in his heart for all this time—it broke her heart.

'You lost a baby too, Gianluca.'

He looked surprised by the comment, as though he had not thought of it that way before.

'It happened.' He flashed a look at her face. 'And you are meant to move on but I didn't. I was so damned terrified of ever being responsible for hurting someone again that I surrounded myself with people as shallow and self-seeking as I am.'

'You're not!' Poppy protested, jumping to her feet.

'I was never going to love anyone, then you came and all those years I'd been thinking about you, thinking about you standing there telling me I was the one you loved, the one who was meant to kiss you, make love to you, and I knew you were right. I just couldn't help myself. You're so delicious and funny and scarily outspoken—I couldn't keep my hands off you. Even though I *knew* no matter what I told myself that I was falling for you and...I never want to hurt you, Poppy, but, God, I am selfish—I need you.'

She flew across the room and straight into his arms. 'The only way you'll hurt me is if you go away again!'

'That's not going to happen,' he said, staring down into the delicate little face turned up to him. Loving every inch of it. 'I'm not that strong. I was going to suggest we take things slowly, give me time to prove...but the baby changes things.'

Poppy lifted a hand to his lips. 'You don't have to prove anything to me, Gianluca. All you have to do is continue loving me.'

'So you will marry me?'

Poppy smiled and thought, *Living the dream.* 'Any time, any place...but not anyone—only you.'

Gianluca's eyes darkened. 'That,' he gasped between

kisses, 'works-for-me. All I need to know is how to get you out of this damned dress. Are you sewn into it or something?'

The complaint made her laugh.

'I've changed my mind!'

In the act of sliding down her zip he froze.

'Not any location—the castle. Everything important, in my life happened there so it only seems right that we—'

He smiled in agreement before seizing the opportunity.

'On one condition.'

She angled a questioning look at his face. 'The next important event in your life will not take place in a remote Scottish castle, it will take place in a hospital ward with all the benefits of modern medicine.'

'I always fancied a home birth...' Seeing his look of horror, she grinned and added, 'But marriage is all about compromise.'

'*Si,*' he slurred, sliding down her zipper to expose the graceful curve of her back. 'But not all, there are other things,' he purred, his mouth brushing her ear lobe.

'Really...that sounds interesting...such as...?'

'I think it would be much easier for me to show you.'

He did.

It was two months to the day later and early evening when Dougal offloaded the last boatload of wedding guests. He took off his waterproofs to reveal his wedding finery and joined them as they walked up to the castle on the boardwalk lined with lights that had been specially constructed for the occasion.

It was one of many new additions that had been

needed to make the castle a suitable venue for the Highland wedding that Gianluca had told his godmother Poppy had set her heart on.

The result of this was that as well as the major structural work required to satisfy the authorities there had been a total renovation of the great hall, and her grandmother now had new plumbing and electrics, the latest in luxury bathrooms and an eco-friendly central-heating system, and all of it achieved without the proud old lady feeling in any way indebted.

The wedding had given her a new lease of life along with her daughter-in-law. Gianluca had made that one simple stipulation—she extended an olive branch or no wedding, because Poppy would not get married without her stepmother present. Millie had managed a lot of the arrangements.

Poppy, a silent observer, had smiled to see him negotiate the deal. It was easy to see why he was so successful, and you had to admire his tactics even if they were upon occasion a bit on the ruthless side.

Still, observing the extraordinary sight earlier that day of her grandmother and Millie collaborating as they oversaw the distribution of the decorative flowers in the great hall, and decided on the sequence the reels should be played in at the ceilidh planned for later, made her grateful that her future husband didn't take no for an answer.

When they had caught her lurking they had both been united again, this time in their disapproval, and despite her protests that it was still too early had chased her away to get ready.

There was no such thing, according to them, as *too*

early when it came to a bride preparing for her big moment.

And it turned out they were right. She had barely set the antique veil in position with the assistance of Dina and her mother when her father knocked on the door.

'It's time, Poppy—are you ready?' he called out.

Poppy turned to her two helpers. 'Am I?' she asked, smoothing the satin skirt of her deceptively simple gown, which hid her tiny bump, with a hand that wasn't quite steady.

Dina clapped her hands and said, 'So cool!'

While Gianluca's sister gave a sigh and said, 'Well, for once my little brother has done something right. You look utterly beautiful.'

'You like?' she asked, opening the door to her father, who promptly burst into manly sobs, which Poppy took to mean yes.

It was Poppy who ended up soothing her emotional father as they made their way to the small private chapel that had last been used when her grandmother had married. As on that occasion, the place was lit by hundreds of candles.

Serene up to that point, she stood poised quite literally on the threshold when the doubts kicked in.

Shaking, she turned to her dad and shook her head. 'I can't do this…it's…getting married, it… Shouldn't I have to take an exam or something? They don't let you drive a car until you've had lessons.'

Behind her some place she heard Dina say, 'Way, way bigger than driving.'

'Be quiet, Dina,' her mother hushed.

Poppy's dad caught both her hands in his. He no longer looked emotional, he looked strong as a rock. 'The only thing you need to ask yourself, Poppy, is—do you love the man? If the answer is yes, sweetie, you don't need any lessons or an exam.'

Of course she did—he was right. Poppy felt her panic slip away to be replaced by an excited sense of anticipation.

'Yes,' she said happily, and then a little louder. 'Yes.'

'Save it for later.'

A single piper played as Poppy walked up the aisle towards Gianluca, who stood waiting resplendent in a kilt to celebrate his Scottish heritage while his grandmother Fiona looked proudly on.

Later Poppy didn't remember the details of the ceremony, but the expression in his eyes as he looked at her would, she knew, stay with her for ever.

When it came to saying yes she had no hesitation.

The reception in the great hall that was lit up with trailing strings of white fairy lights and scented with hundreds and thousands of white roses—not the sort that came with long stems and no scent, but richly fragranced, overblown garden roses—was a lively, boisterous occasion.

It carried on long after Luca put a hand on her shoulder and whispered, 'Time to go, I think,' in her ear.

They slipped away unnoticed. Gianluca locked and bolted the door at the bottom of the stone spiral that led up to the tower bedroom where they were spending their first night as a married couple.

Gianluca undressed her by the light of the moon shining through the window, his eloquent eyes fulfilling the promise he had just made to worship as he bared her pale body.

He kissed until no inch of her tingling skin felt unloved, then he carried her and laid her tenderly on the bed. Undressing quickly, he joined her.

She shivered; his magnificent body tinged with moon silver looked magnificent. 'So, it's true what they say about Scotsmen and kilts?'

'I've not the faintest idea, *cara*, but Italian men view these matters practically. I was thinking easy access—you are sometimes very impatient.' His throaty laughter made the goose bumps rise on her scalp. 'Are you blushing…?'

'You'll have to do better than that if you want to see me blush, Luca Ranieri.'

In the moonlight Luca, who always rose to a challenge, grinned. 'I can do better, a lot better.'

The throaty promise made Poppy smile because she knew he could. 'Show me,' she whispered in his ear.

And he did.

* * * * *

Mills & Boon® Hard Back

December 2011

ROMANCE

Jewel in His Crown	Lynne Graham
The Man Every Woman Wants	Miranda Lee
Once a Ferrara Wife...	Sarah Morgan
Not Fit for a King?	Jane Porter
In Bed with a Stranger	India Grey
In a Storm of Scandal	Kim Lawrence
The Call of the Desert	Abby Green
Playing His Dangerous Game	Tina Duncan
How to Win the Dating War	Aimee Carson
Interview with the Daredevil	Nicola Marsh
Snowbound with Her Hero	Rebecca Winters
The Playboy's Gift	Teresa Carpenter
The Tycoon Who Healed Her Heart	Melissa James
Firefighter Under the Mistletoe	Melissa McClone
Flirting with Italian	Liz Fielding
The Inconvenient Laws of Attraction	Trish Wylie
The Night Before Christmas	Alison Roberts
Once a Good Girl...	Wendy S. Marcus

HISTORICAL

The Disappearing Duchess	Anne Herries
Improper Miss Darling	Gail Whitiker
Beauty and the Scarred Hero	Emily May
Butterfly Swords	Jeannie Lin

MEDICAL ROMANCE™

New Doc in Town	Meredith Webber
Orphan Under the Christmas Tree	Meredith Webber
Surgeon in a Wedding Dress	Sue MacKay
The Boy Who Made Them Love Again	Scarlet Wilson

ROMANCE

Bride for Real — Lynne Graham
From Dirt to Diamonds — Julia James
The Thorn in His Side — Kim Lawrence
Fiancée for One Night — Trish Morey
Australia's Maverick Millionaire — Margaret Way
Rescued by the Brooding Tycoon — Lucy Gordon
Swept Off Her Stilettos — Fiona Harper
Mr Right There All Along — Jackie Braun

HISTORICAL

Ravished by the Rake — Louise Allen
The Rake of Hollowhurst Castle — Elizabeth Beacon
Bought for the Harem — Anne Herries
Slave Princess — Juliet Landon

MEDICAL ROMANCE™

Flirting with the Society Doctor — Janice Lynn
When One Night Isn't Enough — Wendy S. Marcus
Melting the Argentine Doctor's Heart — Meredith Webber
Small Town Marriage Miracle — Jennifer Taylor
St Piran's: Prince on the Children's Ward — Sarah Morgan
Harry St Clair: Rogue or Doctor? — Fiona McArthur

Mills & Boon® Hardback

January 2012

ROMANCE

The Man Who Risked It All	Michelle Reid
The Sheikh's Undoing	Sharon Kendrick
The End of her Innocence	Sara Craven
The Talk of Hollywood	Carole Mortimer
Secrets of Castillo del Arco	Trish Morey
Hajar's Hidden Legacy	Maisey Yates
Untouched by His Diamonds	Lucy Ellis
The Secret Sinclair	Cathy Williams
First Time Lucky?	Natalie Anderson
Say It With Diamonds	Lucy King
Master of the Outback	Margaret Way
The Reluctant Princess	Raye Morgan
Daring to Date the Boss	Barbara Wallace
Their Miracle Twins	Nikki Logan
Runaway Bride	Barbara Hannay
We'll Always Have Paris	Jessica Hart
Heart Surgeon, Hero...Husband?	Susan Carlisle
Doctor's Guide to Dating in the Jungle	Tina Beckett

HISTORICAL

The Mysterious Lord Marlowe	Anne Herries
Marrying the Royal Marine	Carla Kelly
A Most Unladylike Adventure	Elizabeth Beacon
Seduced by Her Highland Warrior	Michelle Willingham

MEDICAL

The Boss She Can't Resist	Lucy Clark
Dr Langley: Protector or Playboy?	Joanna Neil
Daredevil and Dr Kate	Leah Martyn
Spring Proposal in Swallowbrook	Abigail Gordon

Mills & Boon® Large Print

January 2012

ROMANCE

The Kanellis Scandal — Michelle Reid
Monarch of the Sands — Sharon Kendrick
One Night in the Orient — Robyn Donald
His Poor Little Rich Girl — Melanie Milburne
From Daredevil to Devoted Daddy — Barbara McMahon
Little Cowgirl Needs a Mum — Patricia Thayer
To Wed a Rancher — Myrna Mackenzie
The Secret Princess — Jessica Hart

HISTORICAL

Seduced by the Scoundrel — Louise Allen
Unmasking the Duke's Mistress — Margaret McPhee
To Catch a Husband... — Sarah Mallory
The Highlander's Redemption — Marguerite Kaye

MEDICAL

The Playboy of Harley Street — Anne Fraser
Doctor on the Red Carpet — Anne Fraser
Just One Last Night... — Amy Andrews
Suddenly Single Sophie — Leonie Knight
The Doctor & the Runaway Heiress — Marion Lennox
The Surgeon She Never Forgot — Melanie Milburne